About the Author

Lana Thompson, currently lives in Durban, on the South African east coast with her husband, children and a completely unmanageable number of pets. She has always had an interest in the paranormal and a life-long dream of writing a book. A prolific reader and avid horror movie enthusiast, who loves to terrorize friends and family alike, by hiding in dark corners, waiting for the perfect time to pounce, a paranormal horror was the obvious choice of book.

Wrath

Lana Thompson

Wrath

Olympia Publishers
London

www.olympiapublishers.com
OLYMPIA PAPERBACK EDITION

Copyright © Lana Thompson 2024

The right of Lana Thompson to be identified as author of this work has been asserted in accordance with sections 77 and 78 of the Copyright, Designs and Patents Act 1988.

All Rights Reserved

No reproduction, copy or transmission of this publication may be made without written permission.
No paragraph of this publication may be reproduced, copied or transmitted save with the written permission of the publisher, or in accordance with the provisions of the Copyright Act 1956 (as amended).

Any person who commits any unauthorised act in relation to this publication may be liable to criminal prosecution and civil claims for damage.

A CIP catalogue record for this title is available from the British Library.

ISBN: 978-1-80074-774-6

This is a work of fiction.
Names, characters, places and incidents originate from the writer's imagination. Any resemblance to actual persons, living or dead, is purely coincidental.

First Published in 2024

Olympia Publishers
Tallis House
2 Tallis Street
London
EC4Y 0AB

Printed in Great Britain

Dedication

Dedicated to my husband Russell, who has always been my biggest support and my three minions, Connor, Madison and Bodhi, without whom this book would have been written much faster.

Chapter 1

November 26th, 1922
Egypt

Having had a hearty English breakfast on the large terrace of the grand hotel in Cairo, in which they were staying, Lord Carnarvon and his daughter, Evelyn, were excited to at last make the journey to the Valley of the Kings. As they travelled to the dig site, they chatted happily about all the possibilities that this auspicious day could bring. Carter, the chief archaeologist at the dig had found something significant, steps leading down to a tomb in the Valley of the Kings. He had immediately contacted his benefactor, Lord Carnarvon, to tell him the exciting news and request that he travel to Egypt as quickly as he could, to be present when they opened the sealed tomb.

"Do you really think that the tomb has been untampered with Mr. Carter?" Evelyn asked, "Even after so many thousands of years and the prevalence of grave robbers destroying everything they could find over the centuries?"

"Yes," answered Carter, with a grin, "My team and I believe the tombs' seal to be intact! Of course, we cannot tell for certain until we enter the tomb, but my guess is, this tomb has been lost in the sands of time and forgotten about."

"Extraordinary!" piped up Lord Carnarvon. "I can hardly wait to get there. It's been damned difficult enough to contain my Evie's excitement since we heard the news. I'll tell you old boy, that voyage at sea felt like we had circumnavigated the globe several times, such was my daughter's and my anticipation of your discovery! Lord only knows I hardly slept a wink last night."

George Herbert, the Fifth Earl of Carnarvon, was a warm and generous man with high principals and integrity. His infectious personality always endearing him to those around him, surprising many people, who at first glance, seeing this tall, statuesque gentleman, assumed that being a Lord, would be stuffy and egotistical. Nothing could be further from the truth. He always made people feel at ease around him and that was one of the qualities that his daughter, Evelyn, always tried to emulate in her day-to-day life. She was proud to be her father's daughter and was always in awe of his ability to speak to anyone from any background and make friends easily. Her father, as well as herself, always spoke to the chimney sweep with as much respect as they would to King George V himself.

Evelyn, beautiful, good-natured and self-assured, was considered tall for a woman of the day and carried herself with dignity. She always took pride in her appearance and attempted to always look her best. With her clothes expertly tailored and fitted to her slim figure and her brunette hair always neatly styled, swept up and away from her face. She was a very attractive woman of twenty-five years.

Laughing and chatting together as they crossed the desert, they surveyed Egypt in all its breath-taking beauty with the desert to one side and the Nile River to the other, the giver of life to many generations of Egyptians since the Pharaohs' times.

This discovery had been many years in the making with many journeys between Egypt and England for Lord Carnarvon over the years, but unfortunately, always with a subsequent disappointment. He had spent many thousands of pounds searching for the elusive burial site of one of the world's most mysterious kings to ever rule.

Finally, standing at the dig site, the trio stepped down towards the tomb. The first thing they saw was a warning, carved into the plaster and stone at the entrance of the tomb...

"Death Shall Come on Swift Wings to Him Who Disturbs the Peace of the King..."

There was just a moment of silence before they brushed it off with a nervous laugh. None of them really believed that there could actually be a curse! That was just to keep the grave robbers at bay, surely? The native Egyptian labourers on site, were not as convinced of the curse's benevolence. As soon as they saw the curse, there were great gasps, as everyone took a step back away from the entrance. Carter, the Earl and his daughter paid them no heed though, they had been dreaming of this day for too long and today, their dreams of this discovery were coming true.

Lord Carnarvon and his daughter looked on, as Carter made a hole in the door. Extending his arm though the hole, holding a flickering candle, Carter had the first glimpse inside.

"Wonderful things!" was Carter's reply when asked what he could see. The tomb was intact and had an amazing array of golden and jewelled treasures along with ancient furniture, wooden chariots, spears and a stone sarcophagus – everything the Pharaoh could ever need in the Afterlife. The sarcophagus contained three gold coffins nested within each other. Within the final one was the mummy of the eighteenth dynasty Pharaoh, Tutankhamen, the nineteen-year-old boy-king who was believed to have been murdered.

Legend had it that the Pharaoh, who had become ruler of Egypt at aged eight or nine, had been murdered by a power-hungry relative, intent on taking the throne for himself. Officially, the story had been that Tutankhamen had been killed in battle and the general consensus in modern times is that he simply died of disease, malaria, along with other ailments, being present in his mummy. The death of the Pharaoh brought about the end of the Thutmoside family line. Subsequently, Tutankhamen, his father Akhenaton, stepmother Nefertiti, his wife Ankhesenamun, half-sisters and other family members were included in a campaign of *damnatio memoriae* against them. His images and cartouches were also erased, spearheaded by Horemheb, the Pharaoh at the time.

It was such an exciting mystery for Ancient Egyptian enthusiasts and Egyptologists alike, that Carter and Carnarvon, along with Evelyn, hoped to find the truth by having the mummy examined by the best experts that money could procure.

Work on the site was time consuming. Cataloguing over five thousand items discovered in the tomb, Carter and his team were meticulous in the recording of their discovery. Hour after hour, day after day, Lord Carnarvon and Evelyn were present each step of the way, enthralled with the vast array of treasures.

After a few days, Evelyn started noticing that a blemish on her father's cheek, presumed to be a harmless insect bite, was starting to look a bit infected.

"Father, that bite on your cheek is looking decidedly nastier by the day! I do think that we should have the hotel doctor see to it!" exclaimed Evelyn.

"No, no, my love, I feel fighting fit and I wouldn't dream of missing out on a single moment of this excavation." smiled

Lord Carnarvon, patting Evelyn's hand affectionately. After a ten-minute debate on the dangers of ignoring ones' health, she eventually agreed to give it a few days before arguing the point any further with her stubborn father. But her growing unease should not have been ignored. All was not well with the Earl.

Over the following days, the blemish became increasingly infected, with Lord Carnarvon suffering raging temperatures. He was soon rushed to the hospital. Two days later, the Earl was dead.

The moment that he took his last breath, all the lights in Cairo blacked out and back in England, at the family seat, Highclere Castle, his favourite dog let out a sudden howl and promptly dropped dead.

The Pharaohs' curse had claimed it's victim.

Chapter 2

October 1st, 1923
Calais, France to Dover, England

The ship that Madeleine was travelling on was magnificent. Truly fit for royalty. The cabins were spacious and luxurious. Her particular cabin's sitting room was furnished in rich burgundy with gold trimmed drapes and chairs of the same decoration, as well as cool to the touch grey marble tabletops resting on ornate golden legs and ball and claw feet. Her bedchamber was a heavenly vision in white and gold, with all the amenities you could wish for.

The deck of the ship was dotted with people enjoying the journey, playing games on deck or simply sitting in the deck chairs, with a drink in hand, chatting with one another.

She spent some time out there, before dinner, sipping a small glass of sherry, happily watching the sun sink below the horizon. It was a beautiful sight, with its brilliant hues of red, gold, orange and cerise. The sea was calm and the ship steady, making this quiet moment one of peace and tranquillity. Unfortunately, this feeling was not to last. Almost as soon as the sun bid them farewell, she heard the first, faraway rumbles of an approaching storm. Within an hour, the storm was almost upon them.

Rocking violently back and forth, the ship groaned and creaked with every motion of the sea.

She saw this angry, approaching storm as a sign of troubling times to come.

"An omen..." she whispered to herself as she stood alone on the ships' deck, watching the dark clouds roll towards her. Everyone else had abandoned the deck to dress for dinner, leaving her there, alone with her thoughts.

She could see the lightning flash through the clouds and hear the low rumble of thunder approaching. The wind swirled around her, tangling the tendrils of her hair, as it loosened from its upswept arrangement.

She had long ago learned to trust her intuition unwaveringly and the weather had always been a trusted advisor as to what was on the horizon for her. She could smell the approaching rain in the air and feel the static electricity on her skin, raising the tiny hairs on her arm. The sky was a strange green hue, peeking through the dark oppressive clouds.

"She comes..." the storm whispered in her ear.

If truth be told, she had had a bad feeling since she had received the letter of invitation from Lady Evelyn Beauchamp, requesting that she leave her home in France and come to Lady Beauchamp's family home, Highclere Castle in Britain, for a week. The devastated daughter of Lord Carnarvon was seeking clarity and above all else, closure, on the sudden death of her beloved father. She had requested that Madeleine conduct a series of séances over the course of the week for her family and their guests that would be in residence at the castle.

She would have preferred to decline the invitation, due to this feeling of sea sickness since the letter arrived, however, Evelyn's letter had been so heartfelt, so sincere, almost pleading for her attendance, that she simply could not refuse.

And so, Madeleine de Longpre, world-renowned psychic

medium and clairvoyant, began making plans for her voyage across the channel. Little did she know at the time, that her life would be forever altered by this trip.

Madeleine hurriedly dressed for dinner in her cabin and made it to the dining room just as the starters were being served. She found her chair at the captains' table. He had invited her to join him, upon boarding the ship. She had suspicions that this was upon the insistence of Lady Evelyn, who had handled her travel arrangements.

Later that evening, after a delicious three-course meal and some delightful chit-chat with the captain and his other V.I.P. guests seated at their table, Madeleine spent some time leisurely getting to know some of the other guests, whilst sipping the fabulous champagne on offer. She decided to go out on deck to observe the passing storm. The weather had been a concern and the psychic message that whispered in the wind had unsettled her. The other guests on the voyage were aware of who she was and what her gift was, so she had made the decision to behave as though nothing was amiss, not wanting to unsettle the other passengers. However, she had ignored the warning long enough and it was time to face whatever was trying to get her attention.

Although it had been threatening to rain for a couple of hours, the storm had simply passed over without the expected rainfall and, out on deck, the full moon had come out to illuminate the night sky, as every star in the universe twinkled with brilliance, she stood in the fresh air, surveying the vast and seemingly endless expanse of the ocean. Lost in thought as to what the next few days had in store for her, she stood in silence as the sounds of the party indoors was in full swing. They would be docking in Dover in the morning and Madeleine would be met by the driver of Highclere Castle to take her to

Lord Carnarvon's family for her week-long stay.

Suddenly, a dark cloud passed over, momentarily eclipsing the moon. The water below turned inky black, where moments before the white horses had playfully skipped along the edges of the waves like slithers of quicksilver in the moonlight. Acutely aware of the lapping of the waves against the side of the boat, it became apparent that she could not hear any of the festivities coming from inside.

It was deathly silent, save for the sound of the ocean. She felt like she was in another time. She heard the cry of a raven... this was indeed an ominous sound, especially since there could not possibly be ravens here in the middle of the ocean. Just as she was starting to question that she'd even heard it, she saw the large dark form of a raven flying low, coming straight towards her. She had to duck out of the way to avoid a collision and just as quickly, it was gone.

Shaken, she stood up to her full height, admittedly only a diminutive five foot and began straightening out her dress, a stunning silver, moon-coloured frock with embroidered detail in silver cotton, when something caught her eye. A few feet away on deck was a woman. She felt a cold chill pass over her as her eyes tried to adjust to the now almost non-existent light. The woman, dressed in a long black dress that was no longer the fashion of the day, was floating in the air. Catching her breath, she gazed into the woman's jet-black eyes that seemed to stare straight into her soul.

Gasping and frozen in terror, Madeleine tried to take in the vision of this woman with the palest white skin, murderous, jet black eyes and lips that looked icy blue. Madeleine could feel the woman's fury oozing out of her and Madeleine was afraid. The woman's long raven coloured hair was floating around her face in wispy tendrils, as if she were under water.

All Madeleine could do was stare at this frightening woman in black, as the apparition flew through the air with astonishing speed and grabbed her arms in her deathly cold hands. As their bodies touched, the woman let out an ear-piercing scream and vanished, leaving behind a dissipating black mist.

What had felt like a lifetime, had just been a few moments and just as suddenly as she had appeared, the clouds shifted away from the moon and its silvery rays bathed Madeleine in light once more. Everything was just as it was before.

Chapter 3

September 24th, 1890
Sicily, Italy

Isabella stood staring at herself in her wedding dress. What should have been the happiest day of her life, her wedding day, had been the unhappiest. Forced to marry a man she did not love.

She had not known Count Vincenzo Francesca for very long, but he had taken an interest in her and had become a frequent visitor to her family's home in the previous few months. Her family had been overjoyed when the Count had requested Isabella's hand in marriage. This would mean the end of their financial worries, but Isabella was horrified! From the time she'd met Vincenzo, she had sensed a nasty side to him, which made her sick with worry. As the wedding day drew closer, he became more and more controlling and possessive of her and wanted to know where she was at all times and with whom.

Of course, she had mentioned nothing of this to her family... she hadn't wanted to upset them as they believed he was a wonderful man who could help them in their time of need. He had a beautiful sprawling villa on Lake Como which he had inherited from his father, the previous Count. He was over twenty years older than Isabella's eighteen years of age and was a self-assured man with a vast fortune in the fishing industry. Vincenzo was a man who was used to getting what he wanted when he wanted it!

Life in Sicily had been difficult for her parents. They had come over from mainland Italy when Isabella was born and had opened a small grocery store in a tiny village overlooking the Mediterranean. They had never had much money, but Isabella had had an idyllic childhood and had grown into a beautiful raven-haired beauty. Dark eyed and olive skinned, people always noticed her when she went by. All the local boys on the island had always been quite smitten with her but she was a good girl and never really took any interest in them.

Just then, her mother walked into the room, "My sweet Isabella, you looked absolutely beautiful today!" she exclaimed with delight, clasping her hands in front of her chest. "Are you happy to be the new Contessa?"

"Oh no Mama, I am not!" sobbed Isabella, turning to face her mother, letting her guard down for the first time, "I do not believe the Count is a good man! He is possessive, rude and nasty when he is not putting on an act for anyone who may be watching!"

"My darling!" exclaimed Isabella's mother, "why did you not say anything to your father and I before? You know that we would never have made you do anything you did not want to do!" A look of concern had etched itself all over her mothers' face.

"I know that Mama, but I think it is best for the family for me to have married him. I don't want you to worry about me, I will be fine and with a little perseverance, I think that the Count will make a fine husband who will take good care of me!" she said, wiping a small tear from her eye. Of course, she didn't truly believe this but had instantly regretted telling her mother of her fears. She did not want her mother and father to worry. Things would be fine, and if it wasn't, she'd just have to make the best of it.

"Come now my Bella, let us get you out of that dress and into more suitable attire for your journey" mama replied, rubbing Isabella's back comfortingly. Isabella's mother was now worried about her daughter but there was nothing that could be done, Isabella was married to this man now and she would just have to pray diligently every night for her daughter to have a happy marriage. "Here is a beautiful dress for you to wear on your adventure to London on your honeymoon" she said, holding up a beautiful deep green dress for Isabella to admire, trying hard to appear upbeat.

"No Mama, I would like to wear one of the black dresses – any of them will do, I don't care" said Isabella, starting to undress. She had already decided that from this day forward, she would wear only black, to mourn her lost freedom. She did not want to make a big fuss of this decision, but somehow it made her feel better that she could at least be in control of what she wore, even if that was the biggest decision she'd ever be required to make.

Dressed in her black, intricately beaded frock with tight corset and full skirt, she made her way downstairs, feeling empowered by the way she looked. She knew that she was beautiful, after all, that was all anyone would ever say to her, how beautiful she was, as if she had nothing more to offer. Her long dark hair was pulled back from her temples to the back of her head with a beautiful ruby clasp. The rest of her hair was left cascading down her back in perfect waves.

"My darling, you look ravishing as always" said the Count with a lecherous grin.

"Thank you," smiled Isabella, forcing herself to be friendly to her new husband. A little annoyed that he hadn't noticed that she was wearing the colour of mourning, she took his outstretched hand to help her into the carriage after saying farewell to her family, she prepared to leave her family home and begin her new life.

Regardless of her feelings for her new husband, Isabella was quite excited to be visiting another country, as she had never left the tiny island of her childhood. At least that was her consolation prize, she thought sadly. And when their honeymoon came to an end in a couple of weeks, she would take up residence at the villa on Lake Como as the new Contessa. Perhaps if she was able to control the Count's temper, she may just enjoy her new life. There was no doubt that he had wanted her as his wife, perhaps, she thought hopefully, that would count for something.

Arriving at the docks, which was only a short distance from her family's home, the boat that they would be sailing on was impressive to say the least. Owned by her new husband, the crew was waiting in a row on the docks to welcome their master and his bride on board.

"Good afternoon, Contessa," said the captain of the ship, bowing and taking her hand in his, lightly brushing his lips to Isabella's hand.

"Good afternoon, Captain. It is lovely to make your acquaintance" smiled Isabella.

"Come along now Isabella, I do not want all these silly niceties to delay us any longer," growled the Count "we haven't got all day to stand here!"

A little shocked at how the Count's temper had flared so quickly, Isabella ascended the stairs onto the boat and turned on the deck to take one last glimpse of the little island where she'd grown up.

"Until we meet again" whispered Isabella.

That evening, Isabella and her new husband had enjoyed a sumptuous meal with the captain as their guest. The Count had seemed agitated during supper and had not seemed to want the captain to pay too much attention to Isabella; however, she had tried to make polite conversation with the captain, so as not to seem rude. She had guessed that the captain had felt the Counts icy demeanour, for as soon as dessert had been consumed, he hurriedly excused himself, saying that he had matters below deck to attend to.

As soon as the captain had taken his leave, the Count turned on Isabella, leaning in close, his face turning from red to purple in a fit of rage, "How dare you embarrass me by flirting with the captain!" he hissed. Isabella was shocked, 'what on earth had brought this on', she wondered.

"I was not flirting at all, just taking an interest in the conversation, my dear," forcing herself to smile but not wanting to make direct eye contact for too long.

Looking into the Count's eyes had always unnerved Isabella. This was certainly one of the reasons that Isabella didn't trust Vincenzo.

She felt it best to stand at this point and try to leave the table, but the Count grabbed her wrist, spit flying from the corners of his mouth as his rage consumed him. "It seems as though I will have to teach you a lesson. No wife of mine will EVER disrespect me!"

Pulling Isabella along by her wrist, he exited the dining room and dragged her with all his might out onto the deck.

He pushed her up against the railings of the boat and leered towards her, a terrified Isabella leaned back and suddenly, the Count shoved her, unable to take control of his aggression. Her foot slipped under her long skirt and accidentally kicked the Count in the shin. This sent him on a rampage; grabbing the hair on the back of her head and hitting her so hard in the face that Isabella lost her hold on the railings and fell overboard. She splashed into the dark sea and swallowed some water. Choking, she screamed for her husband's help, but he just stood there, with the ruby clasp from her hair in his hand, watching Isabella's long black dress, now heavy with water, drag her down into the depths of the ocean.

The Count waited until he could no longer see Isabella on the surface of the water and then he called for help.

"Captain, Captain!" he shouted, "the Contessa has slipped and fallen in the water!" The Count was still full of rage, but he knew how that would look and although he hadn't meant for Isabella to go overboard, once she had, he'd decided to let her drown and be done with her. This was the perfect excuse to get rid of her because he was not at all pleased that she had had the audacity to question him, and so quickly after being married! He knew he really hadn't given Isabella a chance and he could possibly have broken her in like one would do with an unruly horse, but fate had played a part and who was he to question fate?

All the crew were on deck in a matter of moments, spanning the entire length of the boat, calling, "Contessa, Contessa!"

There was no answer…

Chapter 4

October 2nd, 1923
Highclere Castle, Newbury, West Berkshire, England

Sitting in the enchanting Secret Garden at Highclere Castle, the three ladies sipped on cups of lavishly sugared tea and nibbled on Scottish shortbread biscuits and light, fluffy scones, slathered in clotted cream and home-made strawberry jam. It was wonderful to sit in the warm, late morning, autumn sunshine. There was a slight chill in the air but that was to be expected at this time of year, although the autumn had been a gloriously mild one. Winter was not too far away now, and the ladies were enjoying this respite from the cold that would soon be upon them.

"When is this woman supposed to be arriving Evelyn?" asked Evelyn's aunt, Camilla, puffing on a pungent cigarillo.

"After lunch, Aunty Camilla." Spluttered Evelyn, choking on the cigar smoke.

Evelyn loved her mother's eccentric sister dearly but wished that she would sometimes tone down her brash mannerisms. Camilla Beresford was very similar in age to her mother, just over a year younger, (Camilla had always been quick to remind her sister that she was the younger one) and they were very similar in looks, however, Evelyn's mother had aged less than the cigar smoking, hooch drinking widow,

Camilla.

"Good! I hope this so-called medium can see into her own future and foretell that we shall not be waiting for her for tea if she is even a moment late! I must keep my strength up, you know!" exclaimed Camilla, still blowing large plumes of smoke into the air and nursing her gin and tonic, which she always insisted was just water! Evelyn and her mother knew better but didn't call her out on it.

"Do try to keep calm Cammie," cooed Evelyn's mother, Almina, fifth Countess of Carnarvon "no-one is asking you to skip tea or indeed, even supper!"

"I'm glad to hear it!" exclaimed Camilla, "Speaking of tea and supper, are we expecting any of the other guests to be arriving today? I just hope there is enough food and drink to go around!"

"Of course there is! Cook is busy this very moment preparing everything for this evening." said Almina flatly; wondering if there was enough food and drink in the whole world to satisfy her sister's appetites for the good things in life.

Trying to stop the brewing argument in its tracks, Evelyn intervened, "We're expecting all our guests to be arriving just after lunch today."

Taking a sip of her tea, Evelyn's mother, Almina, picked up on her daughter's course of distraction of Camilla. "You realise that Alfred Snowdon will be here this afternoon and you know what he's like with you, especially since Malcolm is away." Said Almina, directing her attention to her daughter.

"Yes, it's a great pity that Alfred's affections cannot be diverted to someone more eligible. He really needs to realise that my marriage is as strong as ever and even if I were not happily married, I have no interest at all in Alfred Snowdon, except as friends", said Evelyn in exasperation. Evelyn and her family had known Alfred Snowdon since her and Alfred were children, snow sledding in the castle grounds in the winter and swimming in the lakes and ponds throughout the summers. Alfred and Evelyn had spent many years together and had been as close as any best friends could have been in those early years. Then, before they knew it, they were all grown up and setting off to university. They had tried to stay close at first, but soon Evelyn had made new friends and didn't have as much time as she used to, to spend with Alfred. Alfred in turn had also been popular at varsity, with many friends and female admirers but had always held a candle for Evelyn. Alfred had always believed that once he and Evelyn were back in their home village, things would fall back into place for the two of them and then, he would make his move and declare his love for Evelyn. Then Evelyn had met Malcolm in her final year of her studies and had fallen hopelessly in love with him. She had taken Malcolm home at the end of that semester to meet her family and soon after graduating from university, they had been married in a glorious ceremony, held at Highclere Castle. Alfred had of course been invited to the wedding and it had taken all his concentration, to act like he was happy for Evelyn and her new husband. Behind the scenes though, he was sick with jealousy and had wished them nothing but unhappiness in their marriage, so that he could step in after the correct period of respect and sweep Evelyn off her feet. Then he would be in his rightful place, by her side, as her husband and they would live happily ever after.

Malcolm was a successful businessman and was away in Europe a few times each year. Alfred would always take this opportunity to try to persuade Evelyn that he was the one for her, always unsuccessfully. Evelyn did not want to hurt Alfred's feelings, but his behaviour was becoming more and more of a challenge for her to ignore.

"I'm sure that he will be respectful of my marriage this time and if he is not, now is the time to put him straight! Malcolm and I have decided to try and start a family in the new year, and I certainly do not want complications from Alfred once there are children in the equation." said Evelyn, rather happily, with babies on her mind.

"That is wonderful news darling," beamed her mother, clapping her hands excitedly, "and I'm sure that if you have a quiet word with Alfred, he will realise his error and be happy for you too!"

"I hope so Mother, I really do, as I don't ever want to hurt Alfred's feelings, but really, he needs to move on with his life now." sighed Evelyn.

"They'll tie you down, those babies will!" said Camilla, grumpy as usual. Evelyn and her mother just glanced at each other and smiled, happily dreaming of babies and grandbabies respectively.

After lunch, Alfred Snowdon was the first guest to arrive, as Evelyn had anticipated.

"Good day, Evie, how are you this fine afternoon?" asked Alfred, grinning at his long-time friend.

"Hello Alfred, I'm very well, thank you. I trust your short trip up the hill was pleasant?" smiled Evelyn. Alfred lived just a short distance away, in the local village, although he and Evelyn didn't see very much of each other nowadays, Evelyn living predominately in London with her husband.

"Very!" Alfred replied, taking Evelyn's hand and kissing it gently.

"Please, do come in and make yourself at home" Evelyn said, linking arms with Alfred as they walked up the stairs and entered the castle. "I've had one of the housekeepers make up your usual guest room; I trust that you will be happy and comfortable there?" she added, "I'll have Rodger take your bags up for you and we can have a small drink in the sitting room if you wish, we have lots of catching up to do!"

"Of course, thank you kindly," said Alfred, leaving his bags for Rodger, the butler, who he'd always thought looked like a decrepit old crow in his black and white uniform. Alfred smiled to himself; some things never change, such as Rodger's virtual lifetime employment with the family. They took good care of him, and the family did not insist on having Rodger perform too many duties anymore in his old age. He simply did not want to leave his post and continued to be up at the crack of dawn to make sure the family were taken care of.

Alfred followed Evelyn to the sitting room on the ground floor which had a magnificent view of the gardens. As they sat together, each having a small whisky, they chatted about this and that event in their lives. Evelyn always found it difficult to confide in Alfred since she got married, as anything she said, Alfred would either get a sad look in his eyes if it were happy news about her and her husband, or he would look smug if the news was not happy, such as news of her husband's frequent business trips to Europe that could not be avoided. Malcolm had many business interests in Europe and that sometimes kept him away from home for a few weeks, several times a year. Evelyn would have liked to always accompany her husband on these trips, but it wasn't always possible, and she realised that once babies had arrived, her chances of getting away with her husband would be that much more difficult to execute. She had aspirations of being a very hands-on mother, involved in every aspect of her future children's lives. Family was very important to Evelyn, and she knew that she would do everything in her power to be the best mother that she could be. Her mother and father had raised her so well and now with her father gone, her mother relied on her enormously, but she wouldn't want it any other way. She sometimes felt the weight of the world on her shoulders in trying to make her mother's life a happy one now that she was widowed, but she realised that at some point, once children came along, her attention on her mother would not be as acute as it was now. This is one of the reasons that she had called Madeleine de Longpre. The whole family needed closure on her father's death, and she felt that her mother would be more able to accept it and perhaps let go of the emotional turmoil of losing her husband, if she had a sign from the other side that he was at peace. Almina was not a woman to show her emotional side, but Evelyn knew her mother well enough to know what was going on behind closed doors. She would often hear her mother sobbing in her room at night, nothing loud and dramatic, just quietly. And the evidence of hours of crying the next day would be etched on Almina's face. If Madeleine de Longpre could ease just a bit of that anguish, then it would be worthwhile. Of course, not all the guests arriving today were as open to spirituality and messages from the "other side" as she and her family were. There were a few sceptics at the gathering that may cause a few hiccups, but she had no doubt that Mademoiselle de Longpre would be able to take it in her stride. After all, that surely went with the job of being a psychic medium?

As the afternoon wore on, more and more guests arrived.

Second to arrive, after Alfred Snowdon, was Henry

Langley, Lord Carnarvon's oldest and dearest friend. Although somewhat senile and more than a little hard of hearing – something he resolutely denied, Henry was a wonderful, kind and caring friend.

"Hello, my darling Mina," said Henry, giving his late best-friend's wife a warm hug.

"Hello darling Henry, how is my favourite man doing today?" smiled Almina, happy in her heart that her friend (a small piece of her husband in some ways) was here now. Henry was much older than herself but was such a warm, loving gentleman that it was hard not to be at peace with the world when he came to visit.

"Very well indeed my dear!" smiled Henry as he ushered Almina indoors.

Just as Evelyn was about to turn indoors as well, having been thoroughly ignored by Henry and her mother, such was their excitement to see each other again, the final guests arrived. Dr and Mrs Foster, the family doctor and coincidentally, the sceptics of the group, although Evelyn was convinced that Mrs Foster just went along with whatever her husband thought about everything. There was no disagreeing with the doctor. He was a stern man who could at times be cruel to his wife, who was no match for her husband's strong personality. Evelyn and Almina often felt pity for Mrs Foster as she was a meek and mild woman who daren't go against her husband's wishes. Camilla on the other hand, had a roaring good time arguing about everything she could think of with the doctor; just to see his colour rise the more he could not get her to agree with him.

"Ah, Evelyn, are you well?" boomed Dr. Foster in his loud and stern voice, with not the slightest hint of a smile, which only ever happened when he was proven right about something.

"Very well, thank you Doctor. Hello Mrs Foster, you are looking well" smiled Evelyn sympathetically at the doctor's wife.

"Thank you" said Mrs Foster, just loud enough to be heard, with a pitiful look on her face. Ah, thought Evelyn to herself, something has transpired on their way here and things are not happy with these two at the moment. She turned and led them indoors, hoping that Mademoiselle de Longpre would be along shortly so that the much-anticipated activities could begin in earnest.

It was a happy feeling for the family to have friends filling up the old place again, she thought, smiling to herself.

Meanwhile, Mademoiselle Madeleine de Longpre was shortly to arrive. She had been accompanied on her journey by the lone raven, since her first encounter with him on deck. She knew that ravens were the harbingers of death, and this fact did not escape her with the raven's constant presence. She realised this must have something to do with the spirit of that woman she had encountered and equally, with whatever awaited her at Highclere Castle.

Finally, her driver pulled up to the castle and it was magnificent. Her thoughts were no longer of bad omens and bringers of death, only magical ideas of olden day times, from the fairy tales her mother used to tell her when she was a child. Growing up in Marseille, France had been wonderful, but Madeleine supposed that most people looked back on their childhoods favourably. She had not realised that she had the gift of clairvoyance until she was seven years old, although subsequently, her mother had told her peculiar stories of strange comments that she would make, about seeing people that were no longer with them in the land of the living, but up until that point, she had had an enchanted upbringing.

Madeleine's mother had married her father, a sailor, to the complete astonishment of Madeleine's grandfather, the wealthy owner of a prosperous vineyard, when she was nineteen years old. It was true that her father never had much money, but he was the kindest man she had ever known and much loved by all who knew him, including her grandfather after he had gotten used to the idea of his only daughter being married to a penniless seaman. Being a sailor meant that her father was away at sea quite often, so her mother and Madeleine, an only child, would pack up a few things and go and stay with her grandmother and grandfather at the vineyard for weeks on end. Madeleine missed her father terribly when he was at sea, but those days at the vineyard were some of the happiest times of her life.

The sun always seemed to shine at the vineyard, and she spent endless days playing in the lush green gardens, courtesy of the intricate water sprinkler system her grandfather needed, to make sure the vineyard thrived. Madeleine spent most days in her own little imaginary world, or helping her grandfather's workers harvest the grapes, although she didn't think she was much help at all, as she ate her way through most of what she had picked.

It was at the vineyard that Madeleine had had her first otherworldly encounter. She still remembered it as if it were yesterday.

After a long day of playing outside in the perpetual sunshine, Madeleine had come into the kitchen of her grandparent's sprawling farmhouse and been ordered by her mother and grandmother to go clean herself up for dinner. She skipped along to the bathroom and ran herself a great big bath of warm water and as a real treat, she sprinkled some of her grandmother's lavender bath salts into the water, after checking that the coast was clear and she wouldn't be caught in the act.

As she lay in the bath with her eyes closed, just her face sticking out of the water, listening to the strange sounds that she could hear with her ears submerged, she felt her stomach lurch. It was a mixture of butterflies in her tummy, like being excited, and something resembling nervousness. It was the first time that she'd ever felt that sensation and it caused her to open her eyes and sit up in the bathtub. She rubbed her eyes with her fingers and blinked a few times as the water from her hair came trickling down onto her face. That's when she saw him for the very first time.

He was standing in the bathroom, just looking at her. She got such a fright that she just froze, all modesty, even at the age of seven, flying out the window, for she didn't even attempt to cover herself up. They just looked at each other for what felt like a lifetime. After what must have been only a few moments, he put his finger up to his lips and said "ssshhhhh" indicating that she shouldn't scream. There was nothing remarkable about this man, other that the fact that he was a stranger, who was standing in the middle of the bathroom. With that, he turned and jumped straight out of the closed window without breaking it. He simply disappeared right through it without a sound and Madeleine was left wondering what had just happened.

She dressed quickly, without bothering to dry herself and walked quickly to her mother in the kitchen, fearing that running would bring about a panic in her that she could not contain. That walk down the hallway towards the kitchen was one of the longest she'd ever walked, as she was fighting the urge to run. Her body was in a cold sweat and her legs felt like lead, all the while trying to ignore her mind screaming "RUN!" As her mother saw the look on her face, she immediately came to Madeleine and asked her what was wrong. Madeleine burst into tears, sobbing and clinging to her mother's skirts.

Madeleine told her what had happened between sobs, as by this stage, she was well and truly gripped in a hold of fear and panic. Her mother's face turned quite pale, and Madeleine could see she didn't really understand what her daughter was saying! She jumped up and ran to the bathroom to inspect, but found nothing, just as Madeleine knew she wouldn't. She came back to the living room where Madeleine's grandmother was trying to console her, her grandfather sitting in the corner, stony-faced. In hindsight, Madeleine believed he'd realised right then and there what was happening to his granddaughter. His family had had a long history of psychic and clairvoyant ability, although this was unknown to the rest of the family, as it was always kept hush hush, like a dirty little secret – the family lunatics seeing ghosts! It always seemed to run in the female line of the family and always skipped a generation, hence Madeleine's mother not inheriting the ability. The only other living relative with the gift was Madeleine's great aunt Fleur, her grandfather's sister, who was labelled the family kook, although Madeleine thought she was wonderful! They shared the same grey eye colour, which no one else in the family had and she was always dressed strangely, like a Romany gypsy, with her gold jewellery and trinkets, jingling and jangling whenever she moved and her many colourful scarves and shawls, draped around her shoulders, her waist or around her head. She was always eyeing Madeleine out like she knew a secret that Madeleine didn't, but that didn't make Madeleine dislike her, she loved being around this strong, slightly crazy old lady whenever she had the chance. Fleur was always making strange statements to people about their lives or secrets they were keeping, but the family would just ignore her when she started "acting up" and put it down to mental illness, which suited the person whom she'd accosted, because what she'd said to them was usually true and always a secret.

Over the years, Madeleine found herself having more and more experiences with the paranormal, which always terrified her. After about six months, she was at the stage of no longer sleeping in her bedroom alone, for fear of the dark shadow man standing in the corner watching her. She was becoming a nervous wreck, seeing things that no one else could. Her mother was at her wits end. She could no longer ignore the situation and all the strange occurrences that were going on, so one day, she went to see the family's local church. Unfortunately, that didn't go at all to plan. She was shut down almost as soon as she mentioned the paranormal and promptly shown the door. Distressed but determined, she went to the local spiritualist society, paranormal phenomena growing rapidly in popularity at the time. They agreed to come and see Madeleine, but over the following weeks, never seemed to have the time to come. Finally, Madeleine's mother went to her parents, to air her frustrations. That's when Madeleine's grandfather told her mother the truth about Fleur and the "gift" that had been passed through the generations to every second female child in the family. Finally, Madeleine's mother felt that they were getting some answers and that's when she immediately contacted Aunty Fleur to come and talk with her daughter.

Fleur and Madeleine became very close over the following years. They spent many an afternoon after school together. Fleur taught her many ways to deal with the occult and enhance her gift, depending on her age and ability at the time. Madeleine was taught palmistry and how to read tarot cards, as well as the softer version, angel cards. She learned how to see visions in the crystal ball and read tea leaves, as well as use the Ouija board, which was strongly discouraged, but Fleur wanted Madeleine to have a broad knowledge of the dark side of the occult too, so that she would be prepared in years to come for any supernatural occurrences. Madeleine was also taught superstitions and their origins and meanings, how to interpret dreams, as well as spells and enchantments of various cultures. The dark arts of black magic were also studied in detail – never to use, only so that Madeleine could spot a curse when presented with one and its corresponding ritual to get rid of it.

By the time Madeleine was eighteen years old, a woman in her own right, she was an accomplished occultist who could spot a charlatan at one hundred paces, of which there were many at the time.

Sadly, just as Fleur had given Madeleine as much knowledge as she possibly could, her dear Aunty Fleur passed away peacefully in her sleep, almost as though through her old age, she had finally done what she needed to do. The night that she died, she came to Madeleine in a dream and asked Madeleine to pass on the knowledge to the next de Longpre in line for the gift, just as she had done for her and to use her gift to make a difference in peoples' lives.

That is the story of how Madeleine came to be where she was that day, climbing out of the car at Highclere Castle. She immediately became aware of her surroundings. The sprawling gardens surrounding the grand building, the late afternoon sunlight reflecting off the castle, making it seem otherworldly; almost painting-like, simply took her breath away. She hoped that she would have time over the coming week to explore a little on her own. She had never seen such splendour and she wanted to take in every inch of it.

Just as the driver was helping her remove her luggage from the car, Evelyn appeared at her side.

Smiling warmly, Evelyn seemed slightly overcome by Madeleine's arrival. "Bonjour Mademoiselle de Longpre, bienvenue" she said, giving Madeleine a friendly embrace as she welcomed her.

"Merci, Lady Beauchamp, I am delighted to be here at your beautiful home" Madeleine replied.

"Oh, this old pile" chuckled Evelyn, looking up at the castle, "rather impressive, isn't it?

"Indeed, it is!" Madeleine smiled.

"Please, come in and meet the family and our guests" said Evelyn, ushering Madeleine inside, "I do hope you'll be comfortable staying with us."

Evelyn had a disarming way of making everyone feel like they were the most important person in the world and Madeleine immediately knew that they would be firm friends.

Entering the drawing room, where everyone had gathered for a few pre-dinner drinks, Evelyn announced Madeleine's arrival. "Attention everyone, I'd like to introduce you to Mademoiselle Madeleine de Longpre" beamed Evelyn, "I hope that everyone will make her stay with us a pleasant one."

"Hello!" everyone chorused, making Madeleine feel most welcome.

Everyone seemed to be in little groups, having various discussions between themselves. Evelyn poured Madeleine a drink and took her around the room to personally introduce her to everyone.

"Mother," called Evelyn, leading Madeleine towards Countess Almina, "please meet our guest of honour! Mademoiselle de Longpre, please meet my mother Almina, Countess of Carnarvon."

"Pleased to meet you, my lady" Madeleine did a small awkward courtesy not really knowing the correct protocol.

"Oh heavens, we don't go for such formality amongst friends my dear! I am so pleased to finally meet you!" said Almina, giving Madeleine the same warm smile as her daughter had done a few moments before.

"Excuse me Countess, I am not familiar with the rules when meeting someone of your great standing" Madeleine grimaced slightly.

"Not at all, let us all just relax and enjoy each other's company without any of that nonsense." Almina reassured her, rubbing her shoulder, in a motherly fashion. "I have heard so much about you and your extraordinary gifts, Mademoiselle de Longpre."

"Please, I must insist that you call me Madeleine, I have no need for formality myself, but thank you for your kind words. I hope that everyone will be pleased with any information and reassurance that I can give once we have conducted the séances. Am I correct in expecting that we will hold a séance every evening, during the course of my stay?" Madeleine enquired.

"That is right," Evelyn chipped in, "however, the first séance will only be done tomorrow night, as we'd like you to get settled first. You have travelled a far way and it is almost six p.m. now, so we will be convening for dinner at eight, once you've had a chance to freshen up and perhaps rest a short while. Tonight, you can take your time and feel at ease with our family and guests and the séances can start tomorrow evening after dinner."

"Thank you, I appreciate your great care of my wellbeing. I am also very much looking forward to discovering all that Highclere Castle has to offer. Your home is very beautiful Countess" Madeleine said, turning to Almina.

"Thank you, child, you are most welcome to take yourself anywhere and everywhere whilst you are staying with us" she said whilst making huge sweeping gestures with her hand.

At that moment, Evelyn turned to Madeleine, "Come along now Madeleine so that I can introduce you to the rest of the group. I'm sure they are all very eager to meet you."

Next, she found herself standing in front of a tall, handsome man. "Madeleine, this is Mr Alfred Snowdon, longtime friend of the family. In fact, Alfred and I grew up together." Smiled Evelyn.

"Good day, Sir" Madeleine said, finding herself quite lost in his beautiful light blue eyes. He had a sadness in his eyes, but they would involuntarily light up whenever he looked at Evelyn. Madeleine could immediately tell that he was in love with Evelyn, but she was sure that Evelyn had previously mentioned a husband in her letter. Madeleine realised that this was the look of unrequited love and she had to admit that she suddenly felt sorry for this Mr Snowdon.

"It is so good to meet you Mademoiselle de Longpre." He said, taking Madeleine's hand and kissing it gently. This man is a romantic, she thought to herself. That can often be dangerous when you add unrequited love to the mix. She smiled graciously at him and was whisked away to the next person she was to meet.

Evelyn steered Madeleine towards an elderly lady, sitting on her own in a wingback chair, quietly nursing the drink in her hand. She was certainly a sturdy woman, and she had an expression of annoyance on her face.

"Aunty Camilla, this is Madeleine de Longpre, the clairvoyant and spirit medium I've been telling you about." The elderly lady looked up into Madeleine's face, but her expression did not change.

"Madeleine, I'd like you to meet my mother's sister, Mrs Camilla Beresford." Madeleine extended her hand towards Camilla, but she did not take it.

"Hello, Mrs Beresford, are you feeling alright?" Madeleine ventured, wondering if the look on her face was her usual expression or that she was unwell.

"Perfectly!" Camilla boomed, "Why wouldn't I be?" she jumped up, out of her chair like a woman half her age, spilling some of her drink in the process. "Oh drat!" she said, looking down at her drink, somewhat unsteadily on her feet.

"Now Aunt Camilla, I think we need to slow down a bit on your water!" said Evelyn calmly, and Madeleine realised at that moment that the liquid in that glass was *not* water and this behaviour was probably a regular occurrence. She smiled to herself; she was going to enjoy the different dynamics at the castle.

At that, Camilla boomed, "Don't be silly Evelyn, it's not water, look at the time, it's drinks hour!" and shuffled off to the drinks trolley to get herself a refill, muttering to herself all the way there.

As they stood there, Evelyn giving Madeleine an apologetic glance, they were joined by Dr and Mrs Foster and the gentleman they had been in conversation with, Mr Henry Langley.

The necessary introductions were made, and Madeleine

found herself instantly drawn to Mrs Foster. From her demeanour she could tell that Mrs Foster had had a hard life and Madeleine could tell by the way her husband spoke to her and answered all Madeleine's questions for his wife, that he was to blame for her quiet, nervous disposition. Mr Langley on the other hand was an utter delight! He was friendly and outgoing, and Madeleine immediately felt her spirits lift around him. She could see why he was such a treasured friend of the late Earl and his family. Although getting on in years, he really was still living life to the full.

Eventually the party broke up and Madeleine was relieved that she could finally be shown to her room. Being in a crowd always made her a bit off-kilter, because for every person present, there were dozens more trying to give her messages for them from the other side. It was rather an exhausting process; however, she ignored the spirits and did not give out any messages, preferring to keep a low profile for the first day at least.

She unpacked and spent some quiet moments freshening up and reflecting on the different characters in the castle. She made a promise to herself that she would try to see a bit of the castle tomorrow morning but right now, she needed to change for dinner, as the dinner bell would be rung in about half an hour.

Madeleine quickly dressed and fixed her hair, examining herself in the mirror. She looked tired and certainly felt that way too. She splashed some water on her face and drank a glass of water. Looking a little perkier, the bell sounded, and she made her way downstairs for the evening.

Dinner had been a gastronomic affair and Madeleine could see herself getting used to this lifestyle. They dined on pheasant and the castle's home-grown vegetables, with trifle for pudding.

All the courses were delicious. They were served various wines and champagne with the different courses and afterwards, everyone retired to the library for after-dinner drinks. The men in the group played a few card games and smoked their cigars and the ladies sat and chatted, drinking their sherry, all except Camilla, who sat with the men and drank what looked like scotch and smoked her cigarillos. She played blackjack with the men and argued with them about the rules and everything else under the sun. It was also clear that she did not like to lose, and Madeleine guessed that the men let her win for the most part, out of sheer exasperation. Madeleine couldn't help but giggle quietly to herself about it all.

Camilla certainly was a force to be reckoned with. Madeleine could tell that despite Camilla's angry demeanour, she was not a mean-spirited person, just practical and no nonsense.

At about ten p.m. Madeleine excused herself after an acceptable amount of time had lapse after dinner and walked up to her room on the second floor. The castle, although light and airy in the day with its many full-length windows, became cold and menacing by night. The only sound as she ascended the grand staircase was the tick tock of the beautifully crafted grandfather clock near the foot of the stairs.

When she reached the top of the staircase, she paused; slightly disorientated as to which side her room was located. She decided it was to the right but took one last look to the left to see if anything jogged her memory from earlier on her way down to the dining room. As she peered into the dimly lit area to her left, there, standing stock still, she could see a dark patch just behind the rail of the balcony towards a door to one of the bedrooms. Madeleine's eyes tried to adjust to the darkness, and she was positive that the light, or lack thereof, was playing tricks on her.

Within a second, this black form seemed to take a step closer, into the lighter part of the passageway and the realisation dawned on Madeleine that it was the woman from the ship's deck that had frightened her almost to death the night before. Madeleine stood as still as a statue and blinked hard a few times, trying to get the image clearer. She caught her breath as she realised the woman was looking directly at Madeleine with her cold dead eyes. She had that same raven that had followed Madeleine all the way to England, perched on her shoulder, also staring directly at Madeleine. Madeleine gasped, stumbling over her own feet and falling slightly against the handrail of the staircase. Madeleine composed herself quickly and as she looked up again in the woman's direction, she and her raven were gone.

Madeleine hurried off to her room as fast as she could walk, knowing if she ran, the panic would set in, and she fought hard to keep it from rising within her. She felt frightened and unsure of what was about to happen when she eventually went into a trance-like state for the séance tomorrow night and indeed, for the rest of her stay here at the castle. She only hoped that she could find the answers to why this woman was pursuing her. She knew that no-one else could have seen the woman in the castle, as nobody had come to Madeleine about it, and surely, she would be the likely person they would confide in.

That whole night Madeleine lay in her bed, constantly seeing a black mist forming in the corner of the room, in her peripheral vision. That is where the spirit world lived, where most people would see something out of the corner of their eye and when they looked, there was nothing, just as was happening to Madeleine now. She must have eventually fallen asleep, as the next thing she knew, it was morning.

At breakfast, Madeleine did not dare mention what she had seen the night before. Everyone was happily discussing what they would be doing for the day and of course, they were all very excited about that evening's scheduled séance. The feeling of dread was creeping up into Madeleine's throat the moment the séance was mentioned. She didn't know anyone here very well and she just hoped that they would be prepared for whatever was to come tonight.

It was a beautiful morning so Madeleine decided she would do as she had planned and explore the castle and grounds for a while.

The sun was shining but there was a chill in the air, so after breakfast, she went up to her room to fetch a light shawl for around her shoulders, in case it got any colder. The wind was coming up, so she knew she would be chilly on the castle grounds, and she didn't want to have to cut her exploration short because she was cold.

She also decided she would need to have a rest later, before dinner, so that she could be in top form for that night's séance.

Madeleine decided her room was the ideal starting point for her little adventure. Closing the door behind her, the hallway was quiet, the other guests all doing whatever was on their agenda for the day.

Madeleine's room was the furthest room from the central staircase, so she made her way towards it. She knew there were just bedrooms on this level and didn't know exactly where everyone was staying yet and didn't want to walk into someone's occupied room. She decided to head downstairs and explore the various ornately decorated rooms.

As she descended the stairs, she looked up to the spot where she had seen the spectre last night.

The apparition was not there, and Madeleine didn't feel any of the heaviness that she had felt the night before upon seeing the woman and her raven. Madeleine took her time going through the castle downstairs and marvelling at how beautifully everything was decorated. The castle was so stylish and elegant, and she could see how proud the family was of their ancestral home. The utmost care had been taken with every detail and although some of the rooms, which the family did not use, had furniture covered with sheets, there were details in every room that fascinated her. She was most taken with the portraits of the family and their ancestors, past Earls of Carnarvon and their wives and children. She loved the fact that there was so much history in this family and that it had been preserved for so many hundreds of years, for generations to come.

Finally, she made her way out into the sunlight. There was a slight buzzing in her ears every so often and she had experienced that inside the castle as well. Now, it was a little more pronounced, but she ignored it.

She spent some time roaming around the gardens, enjoying the beauty surrounding her and slowly made her way back towards the castle.

Madeleine walked along the gravel drive and noticed the lake, with a small pavilion nestled close beside it. Painted white with some pretty, brightly coloured flowers and a couple of chairs facing the lake, she took a seat upon entering and took in the stunning scenery. It was breath-taking and she was so happy to be alone there, in the peace and quiet, feeling so tranquil and breathing in the fresh, clean, country air. She closed her eyes and sat for a few moments, before becoming aware of the buzzing in her ears again, this time louder than before. All the birdsong and crickets had ceased and all she could hear was that damned buzzing.

Opening her eyes slowly, she looked out over the lake. There was the apparition. Floating *above* the water. Her skirts and dark hair afloat around her and her eyes – completely black and trained directly on Madeleine. Madeleine's heart was beating fast, and it felt like it was sitting in her throat. Madeleine forced herself to calm down. Just then, the apparition's raven flew overhead, and Madeleine heard its cry. It flew directly to the woman and she lifted her hand, upon which it landed and jumped slowly onto her shoulder. Madeleine could feel the anger emanating from the woman and she knew this apparition was hell bent, but on what? What could she want from Madeleine? Did she need help? Or was it the family and castle which drew her here, but that didn't make any sense, she had followed *Madeleine* all this way!

With these questions racing through Madeleine's mind, she heard the first rumble of thunder, the wind suddenly blowing furiously and right before Madeleine's eyes, the apparition slowly faded away. Madeleine was not sure how long she had sat there for, it had seemed like only a few minutes but when she looked at her pocket watch, it showed that it was already almost dinner time! She had been there for hours and completely missed lunch and afternoon tea!

Madeleine gathered her shawl tightly around her shoulders against the brewing thunderstorm and made for the castle as fast as she could. She had wanted to rest a while before dinner, but she would have to dress quickly and make her way down to the dining hall.

"My goodness gracious, Madeleine, we've been wondering where you'd disappeared to!" exclaimed Evelyn in the dining hall.

"My apologies," Madeleine stammered, taking her seat next to Evelyn, "I lost track of time in the grounds."

"You must be famished" she laughed.

"I am! I didn't realise how long I had been out and haven't had a bite to eat or anything to drink since breakfast!" she responded, trying to forget the reason she was late and wondering if she was looking as dishevelled as she felt.

Dinner passed the same way as the night before, in relative merriment with light conversation, although Madeleine had the distinct feeling that the guests were getting a little nervous about the séance that night, as no-one mentioned it throughout dinner. Almost as though she had read Madeleine's mind, Evelyn raised herself to her feet and announced that the séance would be convening shortly and that she'd like everyone in the group to meet in the library.

Nervous for the first time ever to conduct a séance, Madeleine immediately went through to the library to gather herself. Evelyn had arranged for the household staff to set up a large round table, big enough to seat them all, in the middle of the room. The room itself was richly decorated in deep reds and gold with dark, wooden furniture. It certainly was a handsome room in which to read the many books which lined all the walls in the room, from floor to ceiling. There was an enormous, elaborate fireplace and there were photos of the late Lord Carnarvon all around the room, as well as historical artefacts from Egypt and many other civilisations from across the globe.

Evelyn had mentioned to Madeleine that she had chosen this room for the séances, as this had been her father's favourite room in the castle, and he had used this as a study later in his life, although his actual study was elsewhere in the castle. He felt at home in this room and spent many an hour in here, reading, researching and sometimes simply relaxing. This was most definitely Lord Carnarvon's sanctuary.

Madeleine sat down and tried to relax, closing her eyes and taking in a few deep breaths. She could hear the buzzing in her ears faintly and she had come to realise that this was the apparition's way of letting Madeleine know that she was close by.

As the guests started to trickle in, Madeleine took Evelyn aside and told her that she would first explain to the guests how she liked to work and what her process was for entering into the trance-like state, which enabled her to communicate with spirit.

"Welcome," Madeleine began, as everyone took their seats, "I would like to go through how I prefer to work and what to expect once I'm in the trance."

She had everyone's undivided attention, except one. Dr Foster was looking decidedly flushed in the face and muttering under his breath. Evelyn had said to Madeleine that if anyone was the sceptic in the group, it would be the doctor. Madeleine decided to ignore him, not wanting to get into a religious debate or having to defend her abilities.

"I will begin by explaining what will happen" she began. "I will light the candles that are placed on the table and in various spots around the library, so that we are able to see each other and anything else which might present itself. I will then put the lights off in the room." she explained. There were a few murmurings and this in fact, brought her to her next point.

"Everyone seated around the table will then join hands and I will require absolute silence as I begin to enter into the trance" she continued, "Please may I ask, that no matter what you hear or see, you are not to let go of anyone's hand at any time during the séance. So, if your nose itches, scratch it now!" That brought on a few giggles from the group assembled.

"I will then request that Lord Carnarvon come forward to speak with us. Once this happens, you will notice a change in me. My eyes are usually closed but there have been occasions when they are open, so don't be alarmed. My voice may also change, as well as my accent, being French in an English castle; I would expect this to happen when the spirit speaks through me," she laughed, as did most of the guests.

"I also have a pen and paper here with me in case the spirit is inaudible, in which case I will write down what the spirit says. Evelyn, may I ask you to read it out to the group as this happens?" Madeleine asked, turning to Evelyn, sitting next to her.

"Of course, I'm happy to help in any way I can." Smiled Evelyn, somewhat nervously.

"You may ask questions, one at a time if you wish, but I cannot hold onto the spirit if it is intent on leaving, so do not be disappointed if your question is not answered. There will be plenty of time over the next week to get everyone's questions answered." Madeleine reassured the group.

"Now, let us begin by lighting these candles and extinguishing the lights" she turned to Evelyn for assistance. Evelyn immediately left her seat and helped Madeleine light the candles. She then went to the electric light switch and flicked it off.

Back in their seats, Madeleine had Evelyn to one side of her and Mr Snowdon to the other. As they took hands, she noticed that Mr Snowdon's hands were clammy and cold, like a dead fish and he had a very limp grip on her hands. Madeleine thought to herself how a man should have a firm grip and dry hands, but she didn't want to jump to conclusions about Mr Snowdon, as it could very well be the séance making him nervous.

Chapter 5

The group was deathly silent as Madeleine closed her eyes and prepared to enter the trance state.

She had placed a metronome on the table, which helped her to quieten her thoughts and bring her mind to a blank. This was all she could hear, the steady tick tock, tick tock. Madeleine always found this slow monotonous sound to be comforting and helped her to focus on the task at hand, this being the reason she used it during her séances.

She began her slow, rhythmic breathing, in and out, in and out, filling her lungs and expelling the air completely through her mouth, before inhaling another full breath through her nose.

Slowly, the sound of the metronome started to fade away into the distance and she could feel her mental state shifting. This feeling was the same as when one astral travelled, which in a sense, she was doing now. She felt like she was lying down and that her feet were raised above her head, the astral plane pulling her in, feet first. It was always an odd sensation, no matter how many times she did it and she could feel herself going, going, going...

"I am calling George Herbert, Fifth Earl of Carnarvon to join us!' Madeleine called out. "Are you here Lord Carnarvon?" There was a little fidgeting from the group, now becoming all too real for some.

Silence.

"Lord Carnarvon, I have your wife and daughter here who

need to speak with you, please come and talk with us for a short while!" she called out again.

Then, the candles began to flicker, like a slight breeze was moving through the room. The group sat silently, waiting for a sign that Lord Carnarvon was with them.

Suddenly, Madeleine felt a shiver and she knew that Lord Carnarvon had joined them. He had entered into Madeleine's body to speak through her. He started to speak, and Madeleine could hear that her voice had changed to a much deeper version of her own. "She comes!" the words flew out of her mouth in a panicked voice. As suddenly as he had arrived, he was gone. Out of Madeleine's body and out of the room. Everyone sat there, looking at each other dumbly as they tried to process what had just happened.

"I'm not sure what that means ladies and gentlemen, but I will try again to contact Lord Carnarvon quickly" Madeleine stammered, trying to get her mind back to that peaceful place again.

The group had started to murmur, and Madeleine saw the doctor turn to his wife and say, "Poppycock!"

His wife's only response was to glance at Madeleine as her face turned bright red with embarrassment at her husband's rudeness.

Madeleine ignored him for the second time that evening and closed her eyes again, feeling the uneasiness rising in her gut. She took a deep breath. As she opened her mouth to call for the Earl, Madeleine stopped dead in her tracks.

She could feel a shift in the energy of the room and again the candles flickered, more violently than before, almost to the point of being extinguished, like a gust of wind had flown into the room, although this was certainly not the case, as all the windows and doors were shut. Madeleine had checked them herself.

She felt something shove her and the room turned icy cold. Her eyes flew open, and they were pure white, no colour, no irises, and no pupils. The group around the table gasped and suddenly, her head jerked back, mouth wide open, facing the ceiling now. Madeleine could feel this icy feeling rising out of her throat and mouth. Forceful like a gale force wind exiting her body. And there *she* was, floating above the table, suspended in her invisible watery prison.

The spirit stared with her dead black eyes at each of the guests in turn, before turning to Madeleine finally.

It was then that Madeleine noticed her black raven was with her, in his usual perch upon her shoulder.

"Hear me now" she spat, pausing for effect, "Before the week is out, every one of you will feel my wrath!" she cursed, spinning around to face each of them before extending her finger towards Mr Snowdon. "YOU!" she cursed, "you will be the first!" Alfred Snowdon sat in stunned silence as his face went deathly pale. "You want what you cannot have, just as he did!" she said, moving towards Alfred, stopping with her face mere inches away from his.

Alfred opened his mouth, but he was paralysed with fear and could not make a sound.

She then turned to Mrs Foster. "And you! Why do you allow THIS" she looked at the doctor seated next to Mrs Foster, "to control you?"

At that, Dr Foster pushed his chair back and jumped to his feet, breaking the circle of hands, exclaiming "What is the meaning of this?" he shouted angrily, looking from the spirit to Madeleine.

That made this terrifying spirit laugh, the most evil sound Madeleine had ever heard in her life. She threw her head back, her laugh getting louder and louder until she simply disappeared into thin air. The screech of her raven, the last thing they heard as he flapped his large black wings and disappeared, just as his dark mistress had done.

"What is the meaning of this!" Dr Foster demanded again, rather than asking the question.

Madeleine had no answers for him.

"We are here to communicate with Lord Carnarvon, against my better judgement, I might add" he continued, looking angrily at his wife, who sat cowering in her chair. "This is an outrage, being threatened and insulted by your trickery!" he spat at Madeleine.

Turning to Evelyn, he said "This woman you have brought here is a charlatan and I have a mind to pack our bags and leave immediately!" he boomed.

"My apologies Doctor," Madeleine began, "I am just as shocked and confused by what just happened as you are! Please do not leave now. Let us all rest and calm down and tomorrow night, perhaps we can find out what is going on at our next séance." she pleaded.

At this, the doctor grabbed his wife's arm and marched her out of the room, slamming the door behind them.

Evelyn got to her feet and turned the lights back on, blowing out the candles on her way back to her seat. "I think it's time for a drink!" she said blankly, heading towards the scotch on the side table and pouring herself a stiff one.

Everyone sat staring at each other in silence, still too dumbfounded by the turn of events to discuss them.

Evelyn duly poured everyone a drink and handed them out

whilst Madeleine tried to make sense of what just happened.

"Please accept my apologies everyone, I am not sure what just happened. I cannot explain it, something like this has never happened in any séance I have ever conducted, but I feel I do need to come clean about something." she stammered. All the guests looked at her expectantly.

"On my journey here across the channel, I encountered this same spirit on board the ship's deck. We were in the middle of the ocean and one minute I was peacefully looking out over the sea and the next, she was there, full of anger and hatred. She grabbed my arms" she said, pulling up her sleeves to show them the black finger mark bruises on her wrists, which she had up until now, tried to ignore. The bruises were turning a nasty purple black and everyone stared at them.

"I have since seen her twice. Once in the castle grounds and once inside, on the staircase. I apologise again for not warning everyone, but I had no idea what was to happen!" Madeleine pleaded, feeling terrible that she had not mentioned anything before.

"Don't fret, my little bird," cooed the Countess Almina," there is no way you could have known."

"She is psychic, is she not?" exclaimed Camilla, looking at each guest individually.

"Camilla, *please*, not now!" snapped Almina at her sister. With that, Camilla shut her mouth, giving her the appearance of a grumpy old bulldog.

"Let us move to the sitting room, where we can all calm down now" said Almina sternly, leaving no room for argument. Taking Madeleine by the hand softly, she led her out of the room and down the hallway.

Henry Langley immediately followed, catching up to the

two women and clucking over Madeleine in a comforting, grandfatherly fashion, with Camilla trailing behind them.

Evelyn looked over to Alfred, who still sat in his seat at the table. "Are you quite alright Alfie?" asked Evelyn, trying to soften the blow of the apparent curse that the spirit had levelled against him.

His face had turned an ash grey now and sweat trickled from his brow. "Uh, yes" he stuttered, still looking stunned. "Listen, let us leave here tonight, right now, just the two of us!" he pleaded, standing and taking Evelyn in his arms, "I love you Evie, I always have, and I always will!" he said, pulling Evelyn closer to him, kissing her on the lips. Evelyn tried to get out of his embrace, but he pulled her in closer and held her tighter, trying to shove his tongue into her mouth, while pulling at her evening dress to get his hand on her thigh.

"Alfred!" Evelyn screamed, finally finding the strength to get out of his grip, "stop that this instant!" she shouted, pushing him away.

"And why should I, Evelyn? You were mine first! I need you and I swear I shall have you!" he spat, looking less and less like the Alfred she had been so close to all these years. He moved towards her again, loosening the bowtie on his tuxedo. He was totally dishevelled and his hair, usually slicked back to perfection, was sticking up in a sweaty mass on his head. His eyes had a crazy look to them, and his pupils were like pinpricks. He tried to grab her by the arm, and she swatted it away from her.

"Enough Alfred!" she said, trying to calm down. "I think it best if you leave, on your own, this very minute!" she told him angrily, incredibly annoyed with his behaviour.

"I think you've had far too much to drink and either you go

to bed this instant and sleep it off or you leave Highclere Castle immediately!" she spat at him, her anger getting the better of her.

"You are making a mistake Evelyn! How can you think that Malcolm could love you more than I?" he pleaded, calming down slightly.

"Alfred, I am a married woman and I'm sorry if this hurts you, but I love my husband, *only* my husband! You need to accept this now or we cannot continue being friends" she said firmly. "I have been very patient with you up to this point, but I have been married for a couple of years now, yet you continue to live in a fantasy world that you and I will be together. We will never be together the way you want us to be – ever!" At that, Evelyn turned on her heels and left the room in search of the others, leaving Alfred alone to stew. Evelyn stopped suddenly and marched back to Alfred, "Furthermore," she shouted at him, "I cannot believe you've brought this up NOW, after what just happened in the séance and that warning you just received!" Again, spinning on her heels she marched out, leaving Alfred just standing there, watching her angrily.

After a few moments, he poured himself another drink and clumped upstairs to his bedchamber to consider his next move, with his only companion being a bottle of whisky that he'd slipped into his jacket pocket from the drinks trolley. He just could not accept that Evelyn belonged to another man, and he certainly didn't care what that stupid ghost had to say either – what a load of utter rubbish. He was sure it was all a ruse, with Evelyn being the mastermind to get him to back off. But it had the opposite effect, he thought to himself. And he wasn't at all sure *how* they had managed their little trick, but it had to be one, after all, ghosts don't really exist! No! This was not going to make him change his mind about Evelyn. Tonight, he would sneak into her bedroom when the rest of the house was asleep and he'd change her mind, and if he couldn't, well that wasn't going to stop him taking what he wanted. He'd waited long enough for her, and he was sick and tired of waiting! He'd just sit here and bide his time and fill the next few hours with some liquid courage!

In the sitting room, Madeleine sat, staring at her drink, whilst the others tried to cheer her up. Unfortunately, they didn't seem to realise that, yes, ghosts lied, but Madeleine really didn't think this warning should be taken lightly, and she wasn't about to do that. The amount of hatred and anger that emanated from this apparition was too intense not to take seriously. After all, it had followed Madeleine all the way from the Channel and she didn't believe it was just for some idle fun for a bored spirit. This spirit was not bored, she was vengeful.

Madeleine needed to find out what was fuelling this spirit's wrath and stop whatever it had planned for Mr Snowdon and Doctor Foster, because she truly believed this spirit would just end up causing a lot of damage for everyone, just as the spirit had foretold – Alfred and the doctor would simply be the first!

"Please excuse me everyone, I think I will retire to my room now, I am very tired and drained and would like to get some rest so that tomorrow, we can see what can be done about this situation we find ourselves in." said Madeleine, getting to her feet.

"I think it would be a good idea for everyone to get some rest! I'll walk you up Madeleine," said Evelyn.

"I'll need to finish my drink, thank you very much!" announced Camilla, flushing with annoyance. She didn't like being told what to do, even if she was feeling tired and would have liked to have retired to bed now, but on principal, she wasn't going to take orders from anyone!

Henry Langley and Almina drained the contents of their glasses and got to their feet.

"Come dear, I'll walk you to your room" Henry said to Almina, taking her by the hand and leading her out the door. Evelyn and Madeleine followed and left Camilla in peace to finish her drink and skulk off to bed alone.

Camilla sat alone, nursing her scotch and pondering the events of the evening. She had always had a healthy scepticism of the occult, but this had been a frightening display tonight. She was ill at ease and although she'd have loved to believe it was utter rubbish, she just couldn't fathom how Madeleine had managed to pull it off, if it was indeed a hoax.

Madeleine and Evelyn ascended the staircase and walked silently past Dr and Mrs Fosters' room. They heard an argument between husband and wife. Well, if truth be told, it was a one-sided argument, as Dr Foster seemed to be doing all the talking, with very little in reply from his wife.

"I cannot believe this utter nonsense!" said the doctor, spit flying from the corners of his mouth. "And you didn't have anything to say when that *thing* accused me of controlling you! You are a useless wife; I don't know *what* possessed me to marry you! You have always been useless!" he shouted, while his wife sat wiping silent tears away with a hanky. She was well aware that outright crying would provoke her husband to continue ridiculing her, convinced that the harder his wife sobbed, the more right he had been – otherwise why would she be feeling so bad. He stared at her angrily, his blood boiling with rage.

Evelyn raised her hand to knock on the door and interrupt this vicious confrontation, but Madeleine stopped her, shaking her head silently. She felt badly for Mrs Foster, and she certainly didn't like hearing this argument, but she knew better than to get involved in marital disputes, unless it was a physical assault, which obviously they were duty bound to intervene. Abused woman, especially verbally abused woman, often made excuses for their husband's bad behaviour and truly believed that they deserved whatever the husband was dishing out *or* that there was no alternative, and that they wouldn't survive without their husband. It was a truly sad thing to see, but women had to take responsibility for their own decisions and Evelyn barging in to the save the day for Mrs Foster would just end up causing embarrassment for her and themselves when she jumped to her husband's defence.

Evelyn stopped immediately, seeming to understand what was going through Madeleine's mind and nodded. Without making a sound and alerting the doctor and his wife to their presence, they slowly crept away from the door and to their own bedrooms.

"Good night, Evelyn, thank you for all your help tonight." Smiled Madeleine meekly.

"Good night my friend, try to get some rest and please don't worry about everything that transpired tonight. Tomorrow we will reassess the situation, so please don't fret!" said Evelyn warmly, holding Madeleine's hand. At that, she turned and walked to her bedroom, situated next to Madeleine's. She usually slept in an altogether different room when she stayed at the castle, but for convenience's sake, she elected to sleep in the room next to Madeleine's for the week, so that she could be close by, should Madeleine need anything. It hadn't occurred to her to mention it to anyone else, only informing her mother, Madeleine and the staff, so that they could find her in the event of anyone needing her. Little did she know that this single, seemingly irrelevant act was to save her. She never in a million years thought that Alfred would come to find her in her private quarters, which was not a very respectable thing to do, nor would she have ever believed that Alfred would harm her in any way imaginable. He was her friend since childhood, there was no way that Alfred would do anything to hurt her, no matter what had happened this evening – Alfred's behaviour tonight was just the drink talking. Washing her face and getting into her bedclothes, Evelyn lay in bed, going over the evening's events in her mind. It had certainly been a terrifying séance to say the least, yet she was happy that contact had in fact been made with her father, even if it was just to warn them of the approaching spirit. She was hopeful that Madeleine would be able to contact him again the next night and perhaps, that other phantom would just leave them in peace now, having scared them almost to death sufficiently and that would be that! If truth be told she hadn't been particularly worried about this other spirit's appearance, until Madeleine had mentioned that she had seen the spirit a few times and of course, seen those nasty bruises on her arms! She was hopeful that things would settle down now and they could get on with the business of contacting her beloved father.

She wished her husband Malcolm was there with her. She knew he was a very busy man and that he didn't particularly enjoy séances or indeed anything supernatural or to do with the occult, but it would be nice to be able to curl up in his arms and feel safe and protected. This would also have prevented Alfred from that disgustingly drunken outburst earlier.

After a short while, she closed her eyes and was soon sleeping soundly.

Chapter 6

It was after one a.m. when the brooding Alfred finally crept out of his room with the intent of going to see Evelyn to convince her of his eternal love.

He hadn't had any sleep at all and was still furious with Evelyn for not seeing his point of view. He was not normally an angry person, but he was getting desperate, and his anger was further fuelled by the many drinks he had consumed in the last few hours.

Slowly, all the while making sure no-one was up and about, he made his way to Evelyn's bedroom. He knew exactly where it was, as it was the same bedroom she'd had since she was a child and she always stayed in that room when she was at Highclere.

He crept silently along the corridor towards her door. The entire household was asleep, and he knew he wouldn't be caught making his way to Evelyn's bedroom. This side of the Castle, the west wing, was reserved for the family's sleeping quarters and there would be no reason at all for him to be down here, away from the guest rooms in the east wing. He knew the only other people sleeping in this wing were Evelyn's mother, Almina and her sister Camilla, both of whom were heavy sleepers and were unlikely to hear anything happening in Evelyn's room. He came to the correct door and put his ear up against it, listening for any movement in the room.

Silence.

Slowly, he reached for the doorknob and turned it, cracking the door open ever so slightly. He peeped around the corner, still too nervous to go barging inside. The room was still. He opened the door a little more and poked his head around the corner. He couldn't believe it, Evelyn wasn't in there, the room completely unoccupied. He flung the door open and barged in, walking past the empty bed and straight towards the closet. He opened it up, feeling more and more confused. The closet was bare, none of Evelyn's clothing or any personal items were stored in it. "For Christ's sake!" he swore under his breath, careful not to make too much noise. "Where in the hell could she be?" His confusion ebbed away and was replaced by the rage that had consumed him earlier that evening. He slammed the closet doors shut, feeling the anger rising and suddenly not caring if anyone heard him. He ran to the bed and picked up one of the pillows, pushing it to his face and screaming into it. Not getting the relief that he thought he would, he threw the pillow back onto the bed and grabbed the bed sheets and threw them to the floor, knocking over a bedside lamp in his tantrum. He looked at the bedside table where the lamp had sat a moment before and saw a photograph of Evelyn and her husband on their wedding day. Next to it was a small glass figurine of a little girl and a lamb, one of Evelyn's childhood trinkets. He picked this up and threw it viciously across the room, where it shattered against the wall. The sound of the breaking glass seemed to snap Alfred out of his rage, and he stood there, breathing heavily and wiping the sweat off his brow and smoothing his hair down again. He listened for anyone approaching to investigate the noise, but nothing stirred in the house. Trying to compose himself, he looked over at the bedside table, with the wedding photograph sitting there, smugly, staring up at him, taunting him over that which he could never have. He grabbed the photograph in its intricate photo frame and marched out the room. Back in the hallway, he closed the door quietly now that he had gotten control of himself once more. What next? he thought to himself. If she was sleeping in one of the other rooms, it would take him all night to find her in this large castle and he wasn't sure exactly who was staying in which rooms. He simply couldn't chance entering someone else's room and being caught looking for her. There was no way he could explain his way out of that.

He resigned himself to the fact that he would just have to give up for tonight and try to find out tomorrow which room she was staying in. Right now, he needed to calm down, but he knew he wouldn't be able to sleep for a while. He needed fresh air, so with the photograph still in his hand, he quietly made his way out of the west wing and out of the family's private quarters, leading from their bedrooms in the long hallway, towards the grand, central staircase in the main living areas of the castle. Then it hit him, he remembered the old tower stairwell in the far side of the castle, which would take him up to the roof and he could walk the battlements, breathing in the cool night air. There was a great, big, full moon out tonight and that would definitely calm him down, as the moon had always done his entire life.

Arriving at the large, oak door that led up to the rooftop, he pulled at the large, iron door handle, heaving as the door slowly opened. It took a few full body-pulls before the heavy door had opened up enough for him to fit through the doorway. He didn't bother to close it again behind him as it was too heavy and he knew he'd be coming back down this way a little later once he was feeling tired enough to go to bed.

Slowly, he ascended the cold, damp stone stairwell. He could smell the mould in there and taking each large, deep step up was beginning to make him feel nauseas after all the alcohol he'd consumed that night. Round and round the stairwell twirled, winding its way up to the top. As he approached the top, which was just coming into view as he rounded the final bend, he thought he could hear ravens squawking up there on the roof. Opening the second large, heavy wooden door, he was finally at his destination. He stepped out into the moonlight that had lit up the entire rooftop, giving it an eerie appearance.

He took a deep breath of the cold, clean air and started to walk the length of the roof silently, lost in his own thoughts of Evelyn and the life they could share together. Gazing at the photograph in his hands, he thought to himself, why oh, why couldn't she just be with me? He'd asked himself that question a million times over the past few years, never finding the courage to tell her directly what he wanted. Until tonight that is. He continued to pace, trying to enjoy the magnificent surroundings on display. The rolling lawns surrounding the castle, the various gardens, formal ones to sit and have tea in and the secret little fairy gardens that himself and Evie used to play hide and seek in as children, and then finally, the bordering woodlands stretching out as far as the eye could see, all illuminated by this glorious moonlight.

Then he heard that squawking again and turned around to see a lone raven waddling behind him, in the same direction. It would have been a comical sight if it hadn't been so creepy. "Shoo! Shoo!" said Alfred, trying to get rid of this macabre little character. It hopped back a couple of times, away from Alfred's flapping hands and then stopped, tilting it's head and watching him with a puzzled look on its face. He tried to shoo it away again but this time it squawked and hopped once towards him. Taken aback, Alfred took a step backwards. The raven hopped forward again, and Alfred stepped back a few more steps. Now Alfred was right on the ledge of the roof, and he turned to look back down to the driveway outside the front of the house. When he looked back at the raven, there standing behind the bird was the woman from the séance! She stood silently staring at him with her head tilted slightly forward in a menacing way. Her eyes, jet black and murderous, penetrating his very soul! Alfred got such a fright at seeing this terrifying apparition that he gasped and lost his balance slightly. He managed to correct himself so that he wouldn't fall right over the edge of the roof, but suddenly, with alarming speed, she sped towards him, floating in mid-air! She lifted her face level with his and her hair flew back and stood on end so that he could see her whole face, mouth wide open in an ear-piercing scream and shoved him over the edge of the roof. Alfred let out a violent scream as he fell over and time seemed to stand still as he fell back onto the driveway below and hit the ground with a loud thud. Gurgling blood, which trickled out of his nose, mouth and ears, the last thing Alfred saw was the woman, standing on the roof, looking down at him with that raven squawking happily on her shoulder.

Madeleine awoke suddenly, feeling feverish, with the buzzing in her ears again. She got up and had a glass of water, trying to settle herself. She walked over to the window and looked out. Everything was quiet and looked as it should. Climbing back in bed, the buzzing was starting to subside, and she closed her eyes and went back to sleep.

A few hours later, Madeleine woke with a start as Evelyn came rushing into her bedroom.

"Madeleine, please, Madeleine, wake up! There's been a terrible accident!" cried Evelyn, between sobs.

"Oh my god, what has happened?" Madeleine asked, with a sinking feeling, her heart pounding in her chest.

"It's Alfred" wailed Evelyn, "he's fallen to his death from the rooftop!" She was wiping her nose as the tears came streaming down her face. She was completely distraught.

"Oh my god, Evelyn, I'm so sorry to hear that!" Madeleine sympathised, taking Evelyn in her arms and holding her for a long while as she sobbed into Madeleine's shoulder.

"Let me get dressed and then we will talk." Madeleine said.

"Okay, thank you Madeleine, I will wait downstairs with a cup of tea ready for you," said Evelyn, leaving the room.

Madeleine dressed quickly and made herself look presentable. She went downstairs immediately to the dining hall to meet Evelyn. Everyone was there, looking sombre and speaking between themselves in hushed tones. They all looked up at her as she entered the room, and she scanned the room for Evelyn. She was sitting with her mother, who was trying to comfort her, the best she could. Madeleine sat down on the unoccupied seat next to them and tried to comfort Evelyn as well. Rodger brought a plate of breakfast for Madeleine, but she didn't feel hungry at all. She looked around the room and everyone was just pushing their food around their plates grimly.

"Oh Madeleine," cried Evelyn, turning to Madeleine.

"Come now my sweet" Madeleine soothed, "tell me what has happened to poor, dear Mr Snowdon."

"We don't know!" Evelyn sobbed quietly, "All we know is that Rodger found the door to the tower ajar, early this morning. He thought that was suspicious and so he made his way up to the roof, but no-one was up there. He just happened to look over the edge and he saw Alfred lying on the driveway. He rushed down to him, but he was already dead," Evelyn wailed.

"We had a terrible fight last night, Madeleine and I'm worried that he has done this to himself! I will never forgive myself if that's true!" she continued, clinging to Madeleine, looking for reassurance.

"No, no, I do not believe that for even a moment; do not forget about the warning at last night's séance. There could be sinister things at work here, but I will be glad to read the tarot cards for you and perhaps we can find out what really happened!" Madeleine offered.

"Oh, yes please!" pleaded Evelyn, seeming to perk up a little.

Madeleine looked over at where Dr Foster was sitting, and he was looking quite pale. She realised that she should never have reminded Evelyn, and in doing so, the whole table about the warning at the séance, even though she was quite sure that Dr Foster was well aware of it! The doctor's wife, Mabel, was rubbing his back and whispering something to him that Madeleine couldn't hear, reassurances, no doubt. As she watched, Dr Foster looked up into her eyes, then suddenly stood up, pushing his chair back to fall on the floor.

"Enough Mabel!" he screamed at his wife, who turned bright scarlet with embarrassment. He turned on his heels and stormed out of the room without another word, leaving his wife to mutter profuse apologies to the rest of the group before scurrying out of the room after her husband. Madeleine really did feel very sorry for Mrs Foster, but she had no time to delay, she had to find out what was going on here before tonight's séance and before any harm could befall anyone else at the castle.

Madeleine knew from her many years of research and discussion with fellow mediums and clairvoyants at the Paranormal Society in Paris, as well as her beloved aunt Fleur, that having the guests simply leave the castle would not destroy the curse placed upon them and they would have to resolve this situation as fast as possible to prevent any more death or injury. How she wished that her friends at the Paranormal Society were here to help her! There was no time to lose, she had to do this quickly and perhaps Evelyn and herself could get some answers from reading the tarot, as well as the séance that night, where Madeleine would try her best to contact Lord Carnarvon for help from the other side as well as draw upon her spirit guides for assistance.

"Let us go now to the castle's library, Evelyn, I do not wish to delay any longer!" Madeleine said, turning to a quietly sobbing Evelyn. Madeleine got up and left the room, with Evelyn trailing behind her.

"Where is the body?" she asked Evelyn as they walked along the corridor.

"Rodger and a few of the gardening staff moved him to the larder until the local police arrive. They are expected any minute now. And of course, being the only doctor in the house, we woke Dr Foster to come attend to Alfred and try to establish time of death and examine the body." answered Evelyn.

"What did the doctor say?" Madeleine asked.

"Just that it looked as though Alfred had died from full body trauma, which would make perfect sense from the fall and that time of death had been at about two a.m." sobbed Evelyn, beginning to cry again.

They finally reached the library and took their seats where they had sat the night before at the séance. Madeleine took out her deck of tarot cards and gave them to Evelyn to shuffle.

She asked Evelyn to choose three cards and put them face down on the table, which she did.

Slowly, Madeleine turned over the first card, the Death card! Evelyn gasped and Madeleine attempted to reassure her. "Don't be alarmed, the Death card often refers to change, and change can be a good thing too!" Evelyn nodded silently.

Madeleine took hold of the second card and flipped it over to reveal the Fool.

And then the third card, The Devil. All Major Arcana, meaning this was fate, meant to be, nothing could be changed.

There was no way Madeleine was even going to start interpreting these cards for Evelyn, they were self-explanatory. Just to be sure, she asked Evelyn to choose one more card. Madeleine took it from her and flipped it over, Judgment. Madeleine wasn't sure what to make of it all, but she knew it was something bad, she could feel it in her bones.

Evelyn sat there looking at Madeleine sorrowfully as Madeleine's mind raced. Perhaps tonight she would use her Ouija board to contact Lord Carnarvon, just in case that dreadful apparition came back. Madeleine was just about to make up some excuse for the cards that had been drawn when there was a knock on the door.

Evelyn quickly attempted to wipe the tears from her face and Madeleine got up and went to the door to see who was there.

Two policemen, in smart black uniforms were standing behind a tall, plain clothed gentleman who turned to face Madeleine when she opened the door. He was a disarmingly handsome man with the most dazzling blue eyes. The man extended his hand to her with a smile, "How do you do Lady

Beauchamp, I am Detective Inspector Alastair King, at your service" he said, bowing his head very quickly as a gesture of respect.

"I'm afraid you are mistaken, sir" Madeleine stuttered through the words, feeling highly embarrassed of the way this man could make her go all gaga at the mere sight of him.

Evelyn came up from the rear, "I am Lady Beauchamp, sir," she said, extending her hand to take his. "This is Mademoiselle Madeleine de Longpre."

"My apologies Lady Beauchamp and Mademoiselle de Longpre, it was silly of me to just assume who you were," he said.

Both ladies just smiled to reassure him that it was alright.

"I'm afraid I have to ask you both about the events of last night leading up to the death of Mr. Snowdon.

"Of course," said Evelyn, "please do come in and take a seat," she motioned to the chairs at the table where they had just been sitting. The Detective Inspector took a seat and Madeleine could see that he noticed the tarot cards spread on the table and as he looked up, their eyes locked for a moment. Blushing slightly, Madeleine quickly pulled all the cards towards her into a pile, feeling very self-conscious.

Evelyn noticed what had happened and tried to explain, "Mademoiselle de Longpre is a physic medium and clairvoyant, Detective Inspector King, and she is spending the week with us here at Highclere Castle."

He nodded as he listened; giving away no signals that he was either appalled or intrigued by this information.

"After the death of my father last year, my mother, Lady Carnarvon and I contacted Mademoiselle de Longpre to come to Highclere and conduct a series of séances for us… to put our minds at ease regarding my father's untimely death," she explained.

"Yes, my condolences my Lady, I read all about the unfortunate business in the newspapers at the time," said the Detective Inspector, looking sympathetically at Evelyn.

"Thank you, sir," said Evelyn, "anyway, it is quite a story to hear of what has gone on over the last few days, I can assure you. I just don't know if you're likely to believe it, actually!" she smiled half-heartedly, Alfred's tragic death springing to the forefront of her mind.

"Alright, well, why don't you tell me all about it and start from the beginning... but before you go on, I will interview the two of you together at this time and then the other guests individually, but we may have to come back to you my Lady and Mademoiselle de Longpre again at a later date, if that is alright with you?" he smiled, looking from Evelyn to Madeleine.

"Of course," Madeleine and Evelyn replied in unison.

"Well, it all began two days ago when all our guests arrived at Highclere for the week-long stay." Evelyn began.

"Pardon my interruption Lady Beauchamp, but would you please be so kind as to give me all the names of the guests and others in residence before you continue?" Detective Inspector King asked.

"Well, there is myself and my mother, Lady Carnarvon, my aunt on my mother's side, Mrs Camilla Beresford. Then of course, there is Mademoiselle de Longpre. Dr & Mrs Foster, Mr Henry Langley and Alfred Snowdon. The only other people here are the servants." said Evelyn, marking everyone off on her fingers.

"I will need those names as well please, my Lady."

"Oh yes, of course, excuse me. There is our butler, Rodger. The cook, Sarah McIntosh and our two housemaids Millie Hughes and Lily Winters – Millie and Lily, quite comical actually, they are always together, great friends those two are." She giggled a little at their rhyming names, feeling almost delirious at being able to find anything funny at a time like this and wondering what the Detective Inspector must be thinking of her. Shock is an awful thing and makes people behave in strange ways. "And that completes our staff compliment here at Highclere, we keep it to a minimum now that there aren't too many of us in the family staying here nowadays."

"Thank you, you may continue your story, my Lady."

"Well, everyone arrived after lunch and settled in that evening. We did not hold any séance that night as everyone was tired from their journeys, especially Mademoiselle de Longpre, who had travelled all the way from France" said Evelyn, looking over warmly at Madeleine.

"The next day, everyone had their own activities planned but after dinner that evening, we held the first, and thus far, only séance," she continued.

The Detective Inspector merely nodded whilst Evelyn told her tale, glancing up at her and Madeleine every so often, whilst taking notes in his little notebook.

Madeleine sat as still as a statue, still quite mesmerised by the handsome stranger. She was by no means the kind of woman prone to falling head over heels for men randomly, but this man, Alistair King, had a strange hold over her, which she had to admit, she found exhilarating.

Evelyn cast a few sideways glances at Madeleine and realised what was happening. 'Oh, my goodness', Evelyn thought to herself, 'Madeleine is completely smitten!'

Just then, Detective Inspector King interrupted Evelyn's inner dialogue.

"Please, feel free to continue at your own pace my Lady, I understand how difficult this must be for you" he said.

"Madeleine, oh, I beg your pardon, Mademoiselle de Longpre, had begun her trance… Oh, please, do you mind ever so much carrying on the story Madeleine," said Evelyn, looking to Madeleine to continue.

"It would be my pleasure" said Madeleine, patting Evelyn's hand for comfort. She could see that Evelyn was getting distressed and wanted to avoid making her feel any worse that she already did.

Looking directly into the detective's eyes, Madeleine continued to tell him what had transpired the day before.

"During my trance, an apparition revealed itself, and foretold of the coming deaths of Mr. Snowdon and Dr Foster."

"I beg your pardon?" stammered Detective Inspector King, looking at her like she was mad.

"Yes, sir, I don't know what else to tell you. All I know is that I have never seen this apparition before this trip but, for reasons unknown to me at present, she first showed herself to me on the deck of the boat, on my journey to Highclere and so far, I have seen her a few times inside the castle, as well as on the grounds." She looked at Mr King, pleading with her eyes for him to believe her, which she didn't think would happen for even a moment.

He stared at Madeleine for a long time, and she began to fidget nervously.

"You must believe Mademoiselle de Longpre, Mr King! She is absolutely telling you the truth – we all saw it at the séance, ask any of the guests and they'll tell you!" Evelyn intervened.

"I will certainly do that Lady Beauchamp," he answered, his eyes never leaving Madeleine's. "Now tell me exactly what this... this apparition said."

Taking over again, Madeleine told him exactly what the spirit had said, that Mr Snowdon wanted what he couldn't have, and that Dr Foster was a bully and a monster to his wife, and they would both pay with their lives.

"I have to be honest with you both, Madeleine and Mr King." said Evelyn, "After everyone had left the library, when the séance had ended, only Alfred and I were left behind. He attacked me and tried to force himself on me, trying to kiss me and get his hand up my skirts." Evelyn admitted sadly. "Of course, I pushed him away and told him that what he wanted, he could never ever have and oh, he didn't like that at all. I stormed off afterwards and didn't see him again until..." she trailed off, "until this morning when our butler, Rodger, found him lying on the drive outside. He was terribly drunk you see, and I can only imagine that he went up to the roof for some air in his drunken state and slipped and fell!"

"You didn't hear Mr Snowdon scream?" the detective asked.

"No, the walls of the castle are very thick, and I can't imagine that anyone would have heard anything, all the bedrooms being on the side opposite to the drive." said Evelyn, wiping away the fresh tears rolling down her cheeks.

"Alright, I'm going to need to talk to the rest of the household now, starting with Rodger." said Detective Inspector King, getting up from his seat and leading the two ladies to the door. "If I may be so bold as to take control of this room, my Lady, and conduct the interviews from here?"

"Of course. I will locate Rodger immediately and send him to see you here," said Evelyn, stepping out of the library.

"Mademoiselle de Longpre," said the detective, lightly brushing her arm with his hand, "Do not venture too far, I may have need of you again to answer further questions."

"Very well," she said and left the room, behind Evelyn.

Evelyn and Madeleine found Rodger in the kitchens, instructing the kitchen staff that they may have an extra person, Detective Inspector King, joining them for lunch. All the staff seemed to be in the kitchen, trying to keep themselves busy, keeping the panic at bay. They were obviously all aware of what had transpired in the séance last night and the incident this morning – staff always being fully aware of everything that happens in such a large household, even when you wanted something to be kept private, it never really turned out that way.

"Rodger, Detective Inspector King would like to interview you now in the library. He will be meeting with everyone in the castle, so please all make yourselves available." Evelyn said, addressing all the staff.

Following the two ladies out of the kitchen, Rodger turned to Evelyn when they were out of earshot from the other staff.

"Madam, I thought you should know..." he spoke in hushed tones, "your usual bedchamber has been disturbed and I know that you were not using it last night. I have left everything as it is, so that you might like to have a look. I will have the cleaning staff attend to it on your command my Lady."

"Oh my, thank you Rodger, I will go up immediately, but I feel you should mention it to Detective Inspector King in your interview and he will advise us further." Said Evelyn, going quite pale in the face.

With that, Rodger continued on towards the Library and

Evelyn and Madeleine took the staircase to her bedroom.

The bedroom was in complete disarray. The bedding was thrown all about the room, the closet doors were standing wide open, although there was nothing in them and a little ceramic trinket was lying shattered near the bed.

"You don't think this was Alfred last night, do you?" Evelyn asked Madeleine, who stood silently for a moment before answering.

"I'm afraid it does look that way," she said, surveying the room.

"Oh, my goodness," said Evelyn, sobbing again now, "he must have come to my bedroom after our altercation last night!" She gasped, taking in the gravity of the situation. "He was not going to give up, was he? Until he had what he wanted, with or without my permission! I cannot believe he would do something like this!"

"I believe you were in more danger than we could ever have imagined Evelyn, I'm sorry to say." Madeleine walked towards Evelyn and hugged her tightly, trying to comfort her, but at this stage, Madeleine could see fear and then anger etched onto Evelyn's face.

"I have been raised to never speak ill of the dead," she said, her face clouding over, "But how dare he come in here and do this! God only knows what he was capable of if he'd found me in here last night!" She was becoming highly agitated now and Madeleine could see the fury in her eyes. "How *DARE* he!"

"Let us calm down." Madeleine tried to soothe her, "nothing good can come of losing our composure now."

Downstairs, Alastair King took his time interviewing each of the household staff members in turn. Going through their stories with a fine-tooth comb. Other than Rodger, no one else at the castle had seen nor heard anything, most of them having retired shortly after dinner had concluded. The castle's staff quarters were below the ground floor, near the kitchen, so it was completely believable that the staff would not have been witness to anything going on. Rodger had mentioned that Lady Beauchamp's bedchamber had been disturbed and Detective Inspector King decided that would need further investigation following the conclusion of this first round of interviews.

He then called for the guests to begin coming though. He decided to question them all at once and if need be, he could focus in on anyone that required further attention.

The guests all assembled in the library along with Camilla and Almina.

Faced with all the eyes in the room trained directly on him, Detective Inspector King nervously cleared his throat.

"Thank you all for coming so swiftly," he began. "I would like you all to tell me about the events that occurred last night, as well as this morning when you came down for breakfast. Perhaps we could go around the room, starting with you Lady Carnarvon."

"Oh course," Almina said, sighing and thinking back on the disastrous last few hours.

"We had had dinner last night and had retired to this very room for the séance with Madeleine de Longpre. My late husband had made an appearance, but no sooner had he warned us that "she" was coming, he disappeared and this... this frightening apparition appeared to all of us at the table!" Almina could hear her voice rising to something resembling hysterics. She took another deep breath and just as she opened her mouth to continue, her sister Camilla, chipped in.

"Detective Inspector King," she boomed in her usual loud,

commanding voice, "my sister is so desperate to hear from her late husband, that she would believe anything that anyone said to her! But I, on the other hand, do not believe a thing that transpired during that so-called séance."

Almina sat quietly, shaking her head at her sister's outburst. When Camilla was in this mood, there was absolutely no arguing with her – no matter what you said, she would shout louder and louder. Better to just let her get it out of her system before trying to continue.

"She is a charlatan, make no mistake!" Camilla continued, staring Detective Inspector King down, just in case he should attempt to argue with her.

"I fully agree!" piped up Dr Foster, "this whole affair is utter nonsense, and I would not be surprised if that woman runs off back to France this very minute while you have your back turned, interviewing us!" His downturned mouth reminded Detective Inspector King of a sulky child throwing a tantrum.

By now, the whole crowd was muttering to each other, and Detective Inspector King could feel the interview on a downhill slide.

"I have something to say," said Henry Langley, raising his hand like a schoolboy.

"Yes, Mr…?" Detective Inspector King started.

"Mr Henry Langley." Henry introduced himself. "I have to admit that I have found Madeleine de Longpre to be a lovely young lady and the events of that séance last night will haunt me for the rest of my remaining days, few as they may be!" The whole room's gaze was on him.

"Furthermore, I do not believe for even one moment that there was any possible way for Madeleine to have deceived us. We were all there, watching her every move. The room was well lit, and she had brought no one with her that could help with any deception. I believe it, old boy, make no mistake!"

Camilla rolled her eyes and groaned, and everyone started their muttering yet again.

"I believe that to be the truth as well, Detective Inspector," said Almina firmly, smiling at Henry.

"Noted, thank you Lady Carnarvon." Detective Inspector King began.

"Dr Foster," he continued, "I believe that along with Mr Alfred Snowdon, you also received a threat?"

"Pure poppycock, I assure you, Detective Inspector King. I am a man of science and am not prone to these delusions that a few of these others have experienced. I have no doubt that the power of suggestion is at play here and that Mr Snowdon, being the weak person that he is, or rather *was*, had gotten his knickers in a knot and caused his own demise purely on the ravings of that lunatic de Longpre." spat Dr Foster, his face going purple with rage.

"Mrs Foster," DI King said, turning his attention to the doctor's wife, "what is your opinion on the matter?"

Blushing immediately, she simply looked down at her hands resting in her lap, whilst her husband answered for her. "She has NO opinion whatsoever on this!" Dr Foster snarled, and Detective Inspector King realised in that moment that there would be no point in trying to coax the doctor's wife to give him any information, her spirit had been crushed by her bully husband many years ago and was too far gone to bring her own personality back now. Detective Inspector King slowly nodded, thinking where he should steer his questioning now.

Finally, he said, "Did anyone hear or see anything abnormal or suspicious after the séance concluded last night?"

The answer was negative from everyone, and Detective Inspector King dismissed them and sat on his own in the library going through his own thoughts. He decided it might be a good idea to interview the guests individually to get some background information from them, although he believed that Mr Snowdon's death was a case of a tragic accident, caused by sheer stupidity in going up to the rooftop whilst intoxicated. He decided he would break for lunch and continue his interviews once everyone had settled down again.

Lunch at the castle was an almost silent affair, with no-one wanting to discuss anything, especially with Detective Inspector King there. There was obviously no rational reason for this, as no-one at the castle was responsible in any way for the death of Alfred Snowdon, but curiously, just having the detective there, dining with them, was cause for feelings of suspicion of each other. During the main course, Detective Inspector King cleared his throat and announced that he would be conducting individual interviews with the family and guests shortly after lunch. Expecting complaints, he was surprised when everyone agreed, resigned to the fact that the detective had a job to do and the more they co-operated now, the quicker it would be over.

The first to be interviewed was Mrs Foster. Her husband striding up to Detective Inspector King once he had requested that the doctor's wife be the first to speak with him. "I'll be accompanying my wife." Doctor Foster stated matter of factly, believing that if he said it with conviction, the detective would not argue with him.

"I'm afraid not Doctor, you wife will have to be interviewed alone."

The Doctor huffed and puffed but kept his mouth shut, seeing that the detective was in no mood for arguments.

Mrs Foster rose from her seat and followed Alastair King to the library.

"Now, Mrs Foster," said Alastair, smiling warmly at Mrs Foster, trying to put this nervous creature at ease. "Can you tell me a bit of background information about yourself please, such as where you live, etc."

Clearing her throat nervously, Mrs Foster began in a soft voice, "My husband and I live in the village here just down the road from the castle. We have a little cottage, and my husband is the village doctor. He has his consulting rooms on the main road."

"And do you have children?" asked Alastair, thinking that the more she got talking about the details of her everyday life, the more she'd relax and be able to discuss the events of the séance and the murder.

"Sadly, we never had any children of our own. My husband has never wanted children, he doesn't particularly like them. It is one of the greatest regrets in my life..." she trailed off sadly.

"Speaking of your husband, how would you describe your relationship with him and his character?" asked Alastair.

Looking a little taken aback by this direct questioning, she said, "My husband is a very clever man, Detective Inspector King, and I'm very lucky to have him. I only wish that I could avoid annoying him quite so much, but I am rather a silly woman I suppose and that does rather tend to anger my husband. I really should learn to be more mindful of his needs!"

Alastair could not believe what he was hearing! Could this woman really believe that she is unworthy of her husband?

"Well, I think that you are delightful Mrs Foster, and you really should give yourself more credit, I am sure that you have been an exemplary wife to the doctor." He said, making a Mona

Lisa type smile play upon her lips and she began to blush.

Alastair continued, "Tell me a bit about the séance last night."

Her eyes widening at the mere mention of the séance. "It was ever so frightening Detective Inspector, if I hadn't seen it with my own two eyes, I'd never believed it!" she exclaimed.

She went on to describe the events of the evening, ending off with the threats to Alfred Snowdon and Doctor Foster.

"I really don't believe that poor Mr Snowdon was murdered by a spirit, and I don't believe that my husband is going to end up with the same fate. I am a god-fearing woman Detective Inspector, and even though I saw this apparition with my own eyes, I cannot believe that God would allow such an abomination to exist, let alone be able to hurt us!"

"Do you think that the apparition everyone encountered was some sort of trickery by Mademoiselle de Longpre?"

"Oh, I just don't know... I don't want to believe that this thing is real, but I saw it and heard it and it was just so terrifyingly real. I really can't see how Mademoiselle de Longpre would have been able to pull off such a trick, but what do I know about psychics and charlatans, I'm just a simple housewife?"

"Thank you for your time, Mrs Foster" said Alastair, rising to his feet and extended his hand to shake hers.

He spent a few hours interviewing the rest of the guests individually, with no more useful information. He sat by himself for a while, going over the alleged events of the previous evening. Madeleine de Longpre intrigued him so much and he couldn't stop thinking about her.

Evelyn's story of Alfred Snowdon's behaviour was also

troubling him. Perhaps if this murder had not occurred, he would be here investigating a different crime this morning. Detective Inspector King went to find Rodger to show him Evelyn's bedchamber, where he had his two policemen stationed outside the door.

Evelyn and Madeleine were sitting in the garden having some tea when Detective Inspector King approached them.

"Any luck with finding out more about what happened Detective Inspector?" asked Evelyn, offering Alastair a chair. He sat down with the ladies and cleared his throat. "I'm afraid there isn't much to go on. It looks as though Mr Snowdon simply took a stroll on the rooftops while intoxicated and stumbled and fell – a fatal error on his part."

"So, it would seem that my work here for the moment is done." he continued. "However, I would ask that you permit me to sit in on your séance tonight."

"Of course," Evelyn replied immediately, believing this would be the perfect opportunity to show Detective Inspector King that she and Madeleine were not just some lunatics who were inclined to flights of fancy and that he could really get a better understanding of how Madeleine worked.

"Thank you, I think it would give me some insight into the whole affair," he said, smiling at both ladies.

Madeleine was happy that Detective Inspector King was going to be staying, but she knew instinctively that he was a sceptic and she just hoped that this beastly apparition would stay away now and let the family hear from Lord Carnarvon, which was why Madeleine had been invited here in the first place. She did not want any more terrifying experiences and wanted to leave here having done her job, by making connection with Evelyn's father.

She didn't like to admit it but whenever Detective Inspector Alastair King was close by, her heart would flutter and skip a beat. She knew there was a powerful connection between them. She had never really fallen in love with anyone in her entire life, but she imagined that this is what it felt like to be in love. She felt nauseas and nervous and excited whenever he was near and the air around him was static.

The trio all went their separate ways then, Evelyn to check on the kitchen staff for dinner that evening, and Detective Inspector King decided to go back into the village to get a change of clothes, upon Evelyn's insistence that he spend the night at the castle after the séance.

Madeleine took the opportunity to walk the grounds and clear her head in the late afternoon sunlight. She was lost in her own thoughts when the buzzing sound began in her ears again. Oh no, she thought to herself, this is not a good sign. She wished that she could make contact with this spirit and find out what her story was. She looked around her and didn't notice anything unusual, no bad weather on the horizon which along with the buzzing, usually heralded the approach of this malicious apparition. She also didn't see or hear that damn raven, so she felt that all was as it should be.

She decided to head inside, up to her room for a lie down before bathing and dressing for dinner. She would need all her wits about her tonight for the séance.

She went upstairs and entered her bedroom. It felt as cold as ice in there, she could actually see her breath escaping her mouth like smoke. She lit the fire in her room's fireplace and opened up the luggage where she kept all her supplies, such as tarot cards, candles, incense, oils, etc. She took out a few crystals that she wanted to place on the séance table tonight to protect herself and the other guests.

Pyrolusite, a powerfully protective stone to help prevent beings from the lower astral realms getting in, such as gremlins, goblins and ghouls. Black Tourmaline for psychic protection and Fire Agate to send negative energy back to where it came from, as well as for psychic protection. These were very powerful aides in Madeleine's arsenal against evil or dangerous spirits and she used them regularly. Unfortunately, she had not used them the previous night and that was something she regretted deeply. She was sure that tonight would be a different experience. Of course, against very powerful spirits, these crystals were not always guaranteed to work but she was willing to try everything within her power to ensure that evil was not present for tonight's séance.

She took her tarot cards out of their black velvet pouch that protected them from picking up negative energies. She held them in her hands for a while, stroking her beloved cards. Tarot cards were a powerful psychic tool, but they needed to operate on her own energy and aura. By holding them in her hands, she maintained their energy and she could feel the cards vibrating ever so slightly. A sure sign that the cards and herself were in tune with each other.

After she'd gone through her little rituals of handling each piece of crystal and infusing her cards with positive energy, she set to work on oiling her candles in preparation for tonight. She lit her incense sticks, which always gave her a feeling of peace and tranquillity before opening her beautifully engraved wooden candle box, that her grandfather had carved for her, and took out the candles she intended to use that night. Four white candles representing purity, truth and sincerity and one black candle to represent protection. Black candles were also often used for more nefarious pursuits, however, any colour candle or magical item could be used for evil, when in the wrong hands.

She oiled the candles lovingly with an infusion of lavender and peppermint oil for their calming, balancing, clear-thinking properties, as she knew that she'd need all her wits about her tonight.

Finally, feeling a bit more relaxed and at peace, she decided to lie down for about an hour before getting ready for dinner. She felt like her icy room was getting colder and colder the longer she occupied it, so she set to work stoking the fire in the beautifully ornate fireplace in her bedroom. It was made of heavy stone slabs with intricate gothic style carvings of gargoyles and Celtic designs. As she looked closer at the carvings, while she stood warming herself by the fire, she could see the tiny details of mermaids, sirens and water nymphs, all beautifully formed, but with menacing expressions upon their faces. She wouldn't lie, the figures were a little unsettling, but she loved the look of the fireplace, nonetheless, having a lifelong penchant for the macabre. She supposed that life thus far and her gift, had something to do with that, or maybe her creator knew what he was doing when he bestowed the gift of foresight and clairvoyance upon her.

As a child, Madeleine had always loved the stories, fables and legends that she would beg her grandmother to tell her. Her grandmother was a wonderful storyteller and just like Madeleine, her grandmother loved the darker, scarier stories. Madeleine and her grandmother were certainly not evil, malicious or even nasty people, they were just so intrigued by the unknown and absolutely loved the thrill of being afraid and nervous while the story was being told. Her grandmother had the most wonderful talent for taking ordinary fairy tales and making them tales of terror and malice. Madeleine always thought that these versions of the stories were probably closer to the truth than the always happy, "good will prevail" stories that other children were being told. Of course, she understood that children needed to hear those stories to make them good people, but she still thought her grandmother's versions were so much fun and her grandmother and her would scare each other senseless with the stories, then spend ages giggling about it afterwards, like their very own private little joke.

Smiling to herself at the thought of her beloved grandmother, she took herself off to the bed, a massive four poster bed without the canopy above. The mattress was so large and fluffy, that it was fit for the princess in the story The Princess and the Pea.

Climbing up, she lay down and closed her eyes, taking in a long, deep breath.

It was still very light outside, and she hadn't drawn the curtains, not wanting to fall into such a deep sleep that she would be groggy and her mind unclear for later.

She lay there for a few minutes with her eyes closed, trying to fall asleep. She could hear the fire flickering, but it felt like the room was started to feel icy again. She could tell that the room was getting darker, even though her eyes were still closed. When she started to shiver, she decided to check if the fire was still lit. She opened her eyes, and the room was very dark and very still. She could barely see the ceiling through the darkness as she lay on the bed. Within moments, she heard a squawk and looked in the direction of the noise. There, sitting on the end of the bed was the raven. He flapped his wings loudly but didn't leave his post. Madeleine was getting that uneasy feeling, but she was trying to remain calm. She looked up again at the ceiling and caught sight of a patch of inky darkness floating above her. She lay paralysed, knowing what was coming. She gripped the bedsheets on either side of her body with white knuckled fists, feeling the terror rising up in her throat. It felt like she had been lying there watching this watery mass for hours, although it had been mere seconds. Slowly, her eyes started adjusting to the dark and she could see the outline of the woman appearing in the spreading mass. Becoming more and more apparent, the figure was floating in the air, appearing as if she were underwater, her dark hair floating around her like black slithering eels. Her face was becoming clearer and clearer, that blue-lipped mouth, her ivory-coloured skin and the most terrifying of all, that basilisk stare with the power to cause death with a single glance. Cold, dead, murderous eyes. It was the eyes that filled Madeleine with fear. They looked directly into your soul. The apparition said not a word, it didn't have to, it knew that it was causing so much fear and panic within Madeleine, that it needn't do a thing other than show itself to her.

 Madeleine tried to calm down and find clues within the way this apparition was showing herself to Madeleine, anything that would give her an idea of who she had been and why she was hell bent on murder here within these castle walls.

 Madeleine tried to speak but could not get a word out, it felt like her heart was in her throat and she was paralysed with fear.

 Madeleine took a long blink and a deep breath. She opened her eyes again and it was closer to her, floating right above her on the bed, their noses almost touching. Madeleine could smell her. A disgusting stench of damp and death. It looked as though the spirit was just as intrigued by Madeleine as she was with her. Madeleine knew there was a story here and she needed to figure out what it was. Everyone in the castle's life depended on it. The woman cocked her head slightly, almost trying to read Madeleine's thoughts, her icy stare never leaving Madeleine's eyes for even a second.

The apparition reached out a cold, damp hand and touched Madeleine on the shoulder. Unable to move, Madeleine braced herself for something terrible to happen, but something strange happened instead. As soon as the apparition's hand touched Madeleine, her whole appearance changed for a split second, and Madeleine found that she was looking up into the face of a beautiful young lady. Dark, glossy hair, olive skin and beautifully kind dark eyes. For one brief moment, Madeleine could feel the terror and loss that this girl had felt at the time of her death. Then, just as suddenly, everything vanished, the apparition and the raven were gone. She sat up on the bed, breathing heavily after this strange yet powerful event.

Madeleine felt so much compassion for the beautiful woman, that she would need to help find out what happened to her and try to put her soul to rest. But there was no time now, she had to get downstairs for the séance.

Feeling sure that they would not get another visit from this apparition tonight, she felt confident that they would be able to get in touch with Lord Carnarvon. How wrong she would be…

Chapter 7

Madeleine, going through the same rituals as the night before, explained how she wanted to work, more for the benefit of Alistair King, who was unaware of what was to take place.

Everyone sat silently and held each other's hands. It was surprising to Madeleine that Dr and Mrs Foster were attending the séance, but she was pleased to see that they were. The doctor didn't look particularly happy, but he was not openly complaining, so she took that as a good sign.

Extinguishing the lights, Madeleine and Evelyn took their seats and each other's hands.

Slowly, as the night before, Madeleine closed her eyes and listened to the slow methodical tick of the metronome.

She called out for Lord Carnarvon. Nothing. Everyone sat in silence, nervously anticipating what was to happen next.

Then slowly, Madeleine opened her eyes and looked at Lady Carnarvon, sitting across from her.

"My darling!" Lord Carnarvon's voice flowing out of Madeleine's mouth.

Lady Carnarvon gasped. "George, is that you?" she asked.

"I am sorry to have kept you waiting my love, I was unable to be of much assistance last night!" Lord Carnarvon answered.

Everyone was sitting with astonished expressions on their faces, not sure whether to believe it.

"I have missed you my dear Almina, and of course, you my darling Evie" he continued. "But I want you to know that I am at peace, and I am happy. Do not shed tears for me, I am with you always."

Sobbing quietly, Lady Carnarvon could not speak. A mix of sadness and relief had overwhelmed her.

"Now a warning," Lord Carnarvon continued, "you need to stop this séance immediately, *she* is here, right behind me and I'm not sure how long I will be able to hold her off..." Suddenly, the voice of Lord Carnarvon trailed off and Madeleine's body seemed to relax. Evelyn tried to wake Madeleine out of her trance, but it was too late. A high-pitched scream rose out of Madeleine's body and suddenly, the apparition was there, not just speaking though Madeleine, but manifesting herself in the middle of the room above them. She turned to Dr Foster and thrust her face right into his. The force of her wrath pushed him over in his chair and then she was gone. Everyone tried to compose themselves, whilst Mrs Foster was trying to help her husband up from the floor.

"Help, something is terribly wrong!" she wailed.

Everyone quickly arose from their seats to find Dr Foster sweating profusely, a look of agony on his ashen face and clutching at his chest.

"Oh my god, he's having a heart attack!" shouted Detective Inspector King, lunging towards the doctor and loosening the doctor's tie and unbuttoning his shirt.

Mrs Foster was beside herself with terror as everyone crowded around Detective Inspector King as he started performing CPR on the doctor.

"I'll send someone for help!" shouted Evelyn, as she raced to the door to find Rodger.

Detective Inspector King worked tirelessly on Dr Foster until help arrived, but it was too late. The doctor was pronounced dead.

All the ladies crowded around a wailing Mrs Foster, trying to console her. The doctor from the nearby village had come as soon as he could but, in the end, all he could do was give Mrs Foster a sedative and put her to bed.

Breathless and sweating, Detective Inspector King sat down at the table again while the local mortuary took Dr Foster's body away. He could fully understand why Dr Foster would have had a heart attack when he did – that apparition was frightening; however, he did not believe that the apparition had killed the doctor, it was simply a case of death by natural causes.

He had no reason to be at the castle any longer and he was happy about that. As much as Madeleine intrigued him, this séance had definitely made him wary of her.

He went to the bedchamber he'd been staying in and packed up his belongings.

Taking his suitcase downstairs, he found Evelyn alone in the entrance hall, having just seen the village doctor on his way.

"Detective Inspector King," she said, walking towards him, "leaving us already?"

"I'm afraid so, my Lady, I have closed both cases and have no reason to stay any longer." he said. "I do think you should refrain from dabbling in the occult from now on," he continued, "I do not think it wise, considering the misfortune of two of your guests."

"I agree, Detective Inspector King," she nodded, "I think it best for everyone involved that there are no more séances," she said, smiling reassuringly at Alastair.

Evelyn had no intention of telling the Detective Inspector that Madeleine and herself had already discussed conducting their own investigation into this apparition and her story. Detective Inspector King didn't need to know what they were up to, but there was definitely a mystery to uncover and they were determined to find out what it was.

Chapter 8

The next day, after having insisted that Mrs Foster stay on with them for a while to convalesce after the shock of losing her husband, Almina and Henry fussed around the widow, making sure she was always comfortable. Whilst the three of them had tea and discussed topics that were designed to keep Mabel's mind off things, Camilla sat in her favourite wingback chair, nursing a drink and staring off into space.

Meanwhile, Madeleine and Evelyn were alone, elsewhere in the castle, preparing to conduct their secret investigation. They needed to find out why this apparition was plaguing them. What was her story? How did she meet her end? Why was she so wrathful?

They were pretty certain that her death had something to do with water – the smell of damp filled your nostrils when she appeared, and it seemed as though she was floating. Her hair was always moving around her head like jet black eels swimming about her face and the skirts of her dress billowed up around her. Every now and then when she spoke, a lone bubble would escape from her ice cold, blue lips. They had also noticed that her dress was old fashioned, a clear clue as to when she had lived.

The two women sat in the library and carefully wrote down all the clues that they had observed during the two séances.

"I wonder," said Evelyn, "if this woman was murdered?"

"That's a very good observation," said Madeleine, "that

would explain why she is so angry. If that were the case, I would say that she was drowned." She told Evelyn everything that had happened the evening before in her room.

"That would make sense, seeing as she's definitely connected to water in some way" nodded Evelyn.

"Do you think that a jealous husband or lover could have done this to her? She seems very angry with men in particular – controlling men, it would seem." Evelyn continued.

"I absolutely agree, I think we have quite a good base to start our investigations. I think we should spend the rest of the afternoon looking for any information about our clues. For instance, we need to put a timeline to her clothing and that will give us a rough date as to when she died." said Madeleine.

"Yes, and from there, we can travel into the village and go through the newspaper archives at the public library to see if there were any articles about murdered or missing woman that perhaps fit her description." agreed Evelyn, suddenly excited about the investigation, now that they had a plan of action.

They sat discussing the case for a while longer until they were summoned for lunch.

Taking their seats in the grand dining hall, Madeleine and Evelyn were pleased to see that Mrs Foster was in better spirits than earlier. She was enjoying a glass of wine during lunch and seemed to be more relaxed than they had ever seen her. Madeleine wondered if that had anything to do with not having her controlling husband around anymore to make her nervous. Her anxiety seemed to have disappeared altogether.

That afternoon, whilst the rest of the family and friends were playing a game of croquet on the castle's lawn, in the beautiful early afternoon sunlight, Madeleine and Evelyn set off for the public library to do their research.

Having agreed that her dress looked to be from around the end of the nineteenth century, they decided to focus their research on that time period.

Scouring old newspapers from over thirty years ago was time consuming and tedious. Aching backs and strained necks and eyes were discussed much between the pair, but their desire to help this tortured soul was more than they could bare. Every time they found something that they thought could be the article they were looking for; something dashed their hopes again and they were left disappointed. The two ladies wondered if this woman's anger was because her body had either never been found, or that her murderer was never punished. Either way, they were determined to find something to help identify who she was.

They spent the entire afternoon at the library, going through article after article to no avail. Eventually, the librarians started making loud and elaborate noises with their keys whilst locking doors in and around the library and the ladies took that as their cue to leave and return the next day.

Perhaps another séance was in order…

Chapter 9

Lake Como, Lombardy, Northern Italy
October 1st, 1923

Sitting on the terrace of his sprawling mansion, high above the waters of Lake Como, Count Vincenzo Francesca watched the sun set over the horizon, contemplating the life he had lived and the choices he had made along the way.

For all his wealth and titles, he had been a very lonely man. He realised now in his seventy-first year, that there were many things that he had done in his life that he was not proud of. His worst regret was Isabella. How could he have done that to her? He could not begin to understand the rage and anger that had engulfed him so much, as to do that to another human being, let alone his young new bride.

Regret and sadness had followed him like a dark cloud above his head from that day so many years ago and was still, to this day, never far from his thoughts. Yes, he had gotten away with his evil deed, and he had gone on to marry again, twice, after Isabella.

He had had three children, who only spoke to him when they wanted money! His life had not been a happy one and he supposed it was karma. He had paid in many ways for his despicable act.

He often thought that he caught glimpses of Isabella over the years, always just out of the corner of his eye or smelled her perfume, just a subtle reminder of her.

Isabella's parents had been distraught when they'd heard the news of her "fall" overboard and they were inconsolable that her body had never been recovered. Not once, did they ever suspect the truth of the events that happened that fateful night. No-one had ever known that he had waited to call for help until he had watched her heavy skirt drag her down into the inky depths of the ocean. Waited until there was no trace of his wife left and then gave the performance of his life, calling the captain of the boat, sweating and panic stricken. No one ever realising that it was all just an act.

In an attempt to atone for his sin, he had taken it upon himself to send her parents money every month until they died, but he knew it could never be enough. He'd spent his life making himself an even wealthier man, but he had always been looking over his shoulder, waiting for someone to come and lock him away for what he'd done. But nobody ever came, and now, sitting here on his own, a lonely and miserable old man, he felt that he had created his own prison for himself, in his heart and in his mind.

Chapter 10

After dinner that evening, Evelyn and Madeleine left everyone enjoying their after-dinner drinks and made their way to the castle library, which had become their unofficial investigation headquarters.

They lit the séance candles and sat down quietly to attempt to contact the spirit and perhaps gather some more clues as to her identity.

Slowly, Madeleine closed her eyes and began to speak in hushed tones, calling on the woman in black to reveal herself.

"Come to us. Come to us now, so that we can help you," she whispered. Silence.

"Is there anyone here who would like to communicate with us? Please, let us help you!"

Just then, all the candles in the room started to flicker. Madeleine and Evelyn squeezed each other's hands, trying to give each other courage.

They could feel a light, barely noticeable breeze start to swirl around them and with every passing moment, it became stronger and stronger until the wind felt like it was likely to blow them over in their chairs. The candles were now extinguished completely, and the two ladies quickly got up to light them again in the pitch-black darkness of the castle library. As soon as the room was illuminated once more, they could smell the familiar damp, musty smell that the spirit always brought with her. The air in the room took on a blueish tinge, as if they were under water. They turned to look at the table where they had been trying to contact the spirit and there, floating above the table was the apparition. The same black dress, the same long, dark hair, loose and floating around her face as if beneath the sea and that same terrifyingly murderous stare from her jet-black eyes, seeming to penetrate their very souls. The spirit did not move, she simply floated there in mid-air, almost waiting for the ladies to make a move or to scream and run from the room. Madeleine and Evelyn stood frozen with fear. Their breath was escaping their bodies like smoke, for the room had turned deathly cold. Breathing hard for what felt like hours, they slowly took the few steps towards the table and the apparition. She watched them without making a sound.

Sitting down slowly so as not to upset the spirit, Madeleine cleared her throat and began to speak to the woman.

"We would like to help you if you will let us. Tell us who you are and what happened to you."

The woman slowly turned her head to give Madeleine her full attention. She suddenly moved towards Madeleine at great speed and grabbed Madeleine's head between her hands and put her face right up to Madeleine's and stared straight into her eyes.

Madeleine was immediately transported to another place and time. She could hear seagulls and smell salty air. She opened her eyes, and she was standing on a boat. She turned to see a man, escorting a young, beautiful woman onto the ramp of the boat. Madeleine tried to call out but no-one seemed to notice. It was then that she realised that she was somehow just a visitor to this time. She was not really there, and she was essentially just watching the events take place.

She took a deep breath and tried to take in as much detail as possible.

The man and woman were now right in front of her, standing on the boat and the man was leaning in, getting right into the woman's face. He was reprimanding her. Telling her not to embarrass him in front of the boat's crew. She was cowering away and looked distressed at this man's behaviour.

Madeleine realised that this woman was the same one who was terrorising them at Highclere Castle, although a vastly different looking woman. The spirit at the castle was terrifying, but this woman here now, was one of the most beautiful women she'd ever seen. Long dark, lustrous hair cascading down her back, with half of it clipped at the back with the most beautiful hair clasp imaginable. She was wearing the same black dress that the spirit was wearing now, but this had a gorgeous sheen to the material, not like the damp, limp dress of the apparition. Her skin was no longer deathly pale, it was olive toned, healthy and full of life. Her eyes were no longer the dead, jet black eyes of the apparition. They were still dark, yes, but a vibrant, warm brown, which reflected kindness, yet sadness, at the same time.

She made a mental note that this couple were wearing wedding bands.

Madeleine watched as the scene played on, seeing the couple at dinner and then, the awful argument and subsequent altercation that happened on the deck of the boat. It ended with the woman being pushed overboard by her husband and landing in the water with a horrifyingly muffled scream, as the water enveloped her into its dark, icy embrace.

She watched on as the husband calmly watched his wife disappear into the inky black waters of the sea. She watched as he waited for his wife to completely disappear under the water. She watched this murderous man run inside for help, when he already knew it was too late to save her.

The boats crew started to run around, shouting and desperately trying to find the woman in the water. The time went on again to a while later and she saw the captain of the boat approach the husband and address him by name, telling him there was no hope left, while he sat, calmly sipping on some warm sherry. The name was Count Francesca. Madeleine had to make sure she remembered that name!

Suddenly, she heard a gut-wrenching scream pierce the sudden silence and her eyes flew open to reveal that she was back in the castle library, the ungodly scream emanating from the entity.

Within a moment, the spirit was gone, and Madeleine looked at Evelyn, who had her hands over her ears, with her eyes tightly shut, in terror.

She now had the clues to this mystery.

She quickly told Evelyn all about her vision and the name of the man who had killed this woman in black.

Tomorrow, their investigation would continue.

Chapter 11

Making their way to the village library as soon as breakfast had been consumed and endless unanswered questions of their nocturnal activities by the rest of the castle's occupants, Evelyn and Madeleine hurriedly made their way back to the village library the following morning.

They knew they'd have to find some proof of the events that Madeleine saw in her vision before Detective Inspector King would take their bizarre story seriously.

They could barely contain their excitement as they once again sat down to go through the newspaper archives and search for the name Count Francesca. To their utter dismay, birth and death records for Count Francesca went back decades and decades and they had to go through every one of them to find the Count Francesca they were looking for, which took them hours and hours, sitting in the stuffy archive room in the library, going through all the dusty old newspapers.

Finally, their patience was rewarded. There was an article in a newspaper dated early October eighteen ninety, which outlined the tragic accidental drowning of the new bride of Count Vincenzo Francesca on the first day of their honeymoon. The story of Vincenzo Francesca, being a very wealthy and powerful Italian Count, on honeymoon with his new bride, Isabella, when the tragedy struck, had made front page news at the time.

She had slipped in a puddle of water on deck, according to

her husband, and had fallen overboard. The distraught Count had frantically tried to get help but sadly, Isabella had sunk beneath the waves and had been lost forever.

Madeleine and Evelyn, having read this version of events, realised immediately that the Count had covered himself well enough with his story, to evade the law and had gotten away with murder.

They continued well into the afternoon, gathering as much information on the Count and his whereabouts as possible, so that they could hand over all this information to Detective Inspector King in the hopes of convincing him to investigate this case fully. They discovered that the Count had a large villa on Lake Como and was a very wealthy and powerful man, albeit, of advanced age, by this stage. They could find no records of a death notice for the Count, which was to them, a relief, as they might never have the chance to bring him to justice for Isabella's murder and hence, never let her spirit rest.

The pair returned to the castle in high spirits, ravenously hungry but elated at their find. In the morning, they would send an urgent request for Detective Inspector King to come to the castle at his earliest convenience.

Having arrived at the castle just in time for dinner, Madeleine and Evelyn joined the rest of the group.

The Countess Almina, Sir Henry, Camilla and Mabel sat quietly chatting, trying to keep the mood light and cheerful for Mabel, especially. Evelyn and Madeleine sat down with the group.

"Well ladies, what have you been busy doing today, we haven't seen you at all?" asked Almina, to her daughter and Madeleine.

Evelyn looked to Madeleine for encouragement and

Madeleine nodded her head, giving Evelyn the go ahead to tell the group their discovery.

"We've been at the town library, Mother."

Everyone immediately turned and looked at the two of them.

Evelyn continued, "We have been researching our ghost." She said flatly.

Mabel dropped her fork to the floor in shock, but quickly recovered, as the servant rushed to her aid to replace it.

"I see…" said Almina calmly, with an unimpressed look upon her face. She really didn't want any more incidents and felt that perhaps, this would stir up more trouble.

"I realise what you must be thinking" said Madeleine, "but I can assure you, we do not want to cause any problems, however, I cannot leave here knowing that this spirit is not at rest. She could very well stay here at the castle and continue to torment you and your family in my absence," explained Madeleine.

"I see your point" said Almina, "and what, pray tell, are you planning to do about this situation?"

Everyone else remained silent, except for Camilla, who was rolling her eyes and grunting her disapproval.

"Well," said Evelyn, once more taking the lead, "we have made some discoveries, which we believe may help the situation."

The group all looked at each other silently and then back to Evelyn and Madeleine.

"We have discovered that there was an Italian Count, called Count Vincenzo Francesca, who married a much younger woman, Isabella, who we believe is our ghost!" exclaimed Evelyn excitedly.

"If reports are to be believed, on their honeymoon, travelling by boat, Isabella slipped on deck and fell overboard and drowned."

"Oh, how very sad!" exclaimed Almina.

"But... Madeleine had a vision, and it seems that the Count actually pushed his new bride overboard in a fit of rage and waited for her to disappear beneath the water, before calling for help!" explained Evelyn.

"It is no wonder that this spirit is vengeful," said Madeleine calmly, "and it could explain why she followed me from the channel to the castle. I must have crossed her resting place and she saw an opportunity to tell her story. I believe the spirits wrath is keeping her trapped in her watery grave and the only way to release her, would be to make sure that her story comes to light."

"As far as we can tell, the Count is still very much alive, living in his Lake Como villa." continued Evelyn, "and we plan to discuss the matter with Detective Inspector King tomorrow morning. We have already summoned him to join us in the morning."

Their evening continued with everyone discussing the tragic death of this woman, with the exception of Camilla, who seemed highly unimpressed, swigging glass after glass of whisky and Mabel, sitting silently, staring at her plate. Eventually, she piped up, "This is why the spirit confronted me about allowing my husband to control me..." she said sadly, "she had had the same thing happen to her."

Everyone silently studied the doctor's wife, also putting the pieces together for the first time.

With that, Sir Henry, always the diplomat, piped up, "Never fear Mrs Foster, if anyone can sort this mess out, it's our

Evie and Madeleine. Its rather an exciting mystery to be solved, I'd say." He said, smiling at Evelyn and Madeleine.

The rest of the evening continued without another mention of the ghost and her story.

The next morning, Madeleine awoke early and sat by her window, gazing upon the beautiful castle surroundings, sipping her tea. She thought about all the events that had happened over the last few days and how far Evelyn and herself had come in the investigation of this apparition. She only hoped that Detective Inspector King would be able and willing to help them bring justice and hopefully peace to this woman's spirit.

There was a soft rap on the door, and she could hear Evelyn calling her name in a slightly more audible tone above a whisper. Madeleine went to the door and opened it immediately, revealing Evelyn still wearing her nightdress and clutching a tray with a pot of tea and croissants for two.

"Good morning Evelyn" she said, smiling at the woman who was fast becoming a firm friend. She felt a sense of warmth and friendship with Evelyn that she hadn't really felt before with anyone else. Her psychic gift did not always afford her the opportunity to make many friends, even in her childhood. She was always a loner, and the other children didn't want to get too close with the "Fille Fantôme" or "Ghost Girl" as they used to call her back on the playground. She had only had one true friend in childhood, a little girl in the same class at school in grade four. Her name was Aimee and she had moved to the school Madeleine attended at the beginning of her grade four year. It was a stroke of luck for Madeleine because it meant that Aimee was 'the new girl' and as often happens in junior school, no one had taken Aimee under their wing and befriended her that first day, except for Madeleine. Aimee was the best friend that Madeleine had ever had, and she was overjoyed that she was finally not alone at school. Sure, after a short period, the other children at school had tried to break up their friendship by telling Aimee all about Madeleine and her strangeness, but that didn't matter to Aimee, she remembered how Madeleine was the only one to make her feel safe and included on her very first day, when kindness and friendship was what she truly needed.

Aimee knew all about Madeleine's gift anyway. From that first day at school when they became friends, they spent all their time together, and discussed everything in their lives, including Madeleine's confession of being able to see and talk to ghosts.

It never worried Aimee that her friend was unique, in fact she always said that one day when they were grey and old and wrinkled and the time came for Aimee to pass away, being that she was six months older, so therefore, would obviously be first to go, according to their nine-year-old logic, she would come to Madeleine in spirit so they could keep in touch.

It was a very sweet sentiment. Unfortunately, it was tragically to become true sooner than they thought.

One Sunday night, Madeleine was in bed, reading stories in the dark, under her bed covers with a torch, because she was supposed to be asleep. She was just starting to feel sleepy when the hair on her arms started to stand on end, this usually was a sign that spirit was close by.

She heard someone whisper her name and it sounded like it was coming from beside her bed.

Slowly, she lifted the covers and peeked out to see who was there.

It was Aimee, standing in her nightdress, right next to

Madeleine's bed. She looked pale and sickly, and her hair was wet and tangled from sweat. She lifted her arm and extended her hand towards Madeleine, without saying a word, but she didn't need to, Madeleine knew this wasn't good. She shouldn't be seeing her best friend in her room late at night like this. She took Aimee's hand and it felt cold and limp. As soon as they touched hands, Aimee slowly faded away. Madeleine burst into tears and ran to her mother, frantically telling her to go and see Aimee's mother immediately. Madeleine's mother was so concerned about her daughter's state of panic, that she agreed to walk the short distance to Aimee's home. When she finally got home, Madeleine's mother confirmed that Aimee had passed away just a few moments before. She had been ill for a few days and had not been at school the previous week, but no one believed it was anything too serious.

Every single night for exactly one year, to the day, Aimee had come to Madeleine. They never really spoke a lot, mostly just sat together on Madeleine's bed, sadly contemplating how this could ever have happened.

After a year of appearing to Aimee, on the last night that Madeleine ever saw her, Aimee had leaned forward and kissed Madeleine on the forehead. She turned and as she walked away from her friend, she slowly disappeared and never came back. Madeleine was distraught, she'd known immediately that that was their last goodbye. She never really got over losing Aimee, but every year on the anniversary of her death, Aimee's presence could be felt, and she'd get the most amazing scent of roses all around her, just out of nowhere and that was a huge comfort for Madeleine, a sign that her friend was still near and most importantly, at peace.

But now, seeing how close she was becoming with Evelyn,

she was happy that she had made another true friend.

She took the tray from Evelyn's hands and placed it onto the small table by the window where she had been seated. They sat for a while having their early morning breakfast and discussing their lives with each other.

Evelyn spoke about her husband and her long friendship with Alfred Snowdon, as well as growing up in the castle and her great love of her ancestral home. Madeleine could see that Evelyn was sad at the tragic passing of Alfred and she tried to comfort her as much as she could.

Madeleine in turn discussed growing up in France and the uncertainty and unhappiness when she first discovered her gift of clairvoyance, as well as her great love for her aunty who had taught her all she knew now about otherworldly things.

After a while, they decided to split up and get ready for the day, both excited and hopeful about Detective Inspector King's visit later that morning.

Evelyn took her leave and Madeleine began her morning ritual of dressing and lighting her incense to focus the mind and calm her spirit in readiness for the day.

Later that morning, Detective Inspector King's arrival at the castle was announced and Madeleine and Evelyn excitedly jumped up to greet the detective inspector.

Looking as dashing and handsome as always, Detective Inspector King greeted the two ladies and they showed him through to the library to discuss their own investigation's results.

"We have the most exciting news, Detective Inspector!" exclaimed Evelyn, excitedly clapping her hands.

"We think we've discovered the identity of our ghost, and more importantly, her murderer!" she continued.

"I beg your pardon?" said Detective Inspector King, looking very confused.

The ladies began to tell their tale about Isabella and the Count. When they'd finished, Detective Inspector King was astonished. How could these two ladies, who by all accounts, were rational people in every sense of the word, despite one being a psychic medium and both believing they were being haunted, expect him to act on this information. Even to suggest to him that he need travel to Italy to interview this Count, years and years after the alleged murder.

He tried to remain calm because he truly liked these two women and it would be rude of him to minimise the work that they'd clearly done to investigate this, however, he could not get around the facts. And the facts were, that he had no jurisdiction in Italy, this was a closed case of accidental drowning, as far as the Italian authorities were concerned and there would be no way in hell that his superiors would allow him to get involved in this. He wouldn't even know how to approach his superiors with this information, without being thrown in the insane asylum.

Very calmly, he explained his situation to Madeleine and Evelyn. "Ladies, I just cannot get involved with this, for the reasons I've just made clear. However, I will make some inquiries on my end and see what information I can pull up. This theory is absurd, but I will admit that I'm intrigued and will therefore, help where I can."

Disappointment was etched all over the faces of Madeleine and Evelyn, but they agreed to give him a few days to get any information he could before they did anything "irrational" as Detective Inspector King had termed their idea of going to Italy themselves and confronting the Count.

Detective Inspector King explained that if there was anything worth investigating, he had a few days leave owed to him and he'd be happy to accompany them to Italy, if he could. "I have a very dear friend in Italy, not far from the area that you wish to visit and as luck would have it, he just happens to be a detective with the police."

"That is amazing, and I know I can speak for both Madeleine and myself, when I say that we are so appreciative of your efforts to help us, where you can." said Evelyn.

Madeleine was quiet. She could not understand why she just couldn't find her words when Detective Inspector King was around. She had a definite crush on the detective and every time she saw him, the butterflies in her tummy went crazy and made her feel a little ill. She felt dizzy and out of control of her own body.

Every time her thoughts turned to the detective inspector, or his name was mentioned, she felt her stomach lurch and she'd never felt this way about anyone before.

Feeling a little disheartened but hopeful, the ladies bid farewell to Detective Inspector King, and he left the castle. Hopefully he would be able to find out some information for them in the next few days.

Chapter 12

A few days passed uneventfully but Madeleine and Evelyn were still on tender hooks about what Detective Inspector King might find out about this case. They nervously waited for him to come back to them, when, finally, he sent word that he would be coming to the castle the next morning with some interesting news.

The atmosphere was electric and the ladies could not contain themselves. They spent the day discussing everything again for the thousandth time and coming up with different scenarios in their minds about what the news was. They hoped and prayed that it was good news, and each went to bed, lying awake for what felt like an eternity, waiting for dawn to break so that they could speak with the detective inspector.

Walking up to the enormous front doors of the castle on a crisp, breezy morning, the detective inspector was very keen to chat with the ladies. He'd found out some very interesting information and he now felt determined to help these two ladies on their quest for truth.

He had had a very intriguing letter back from his friend in Italy. Massimo Furnarello had said that he had done some research on the incident in the police archives and that although the detectives had felt that Count Vincenzo's version of events had not held up on closer inspection, they had had no evidence of foul play and could not have secured a conviction if they had arrested him.

Massimo said that there was a retired policeman living in a village close to his own home, that had been one of the lead investigators on the case and perhaps, if Alastair and the ladies would like to come to Italy for a few days, he could take them to meet with the man. Perhaps he could shed more light on the case and his gut instincts about what he thought might have happened.

And as a matter of interest, Massimo could also take them to the grave of the young woman who had drowned. The cemetery was not far from the Count's home on Lake Como. Although the woman's body had never been recovered, the Count, at the insistence of his late wife's parents, had erected a tombstone for Isabella. He refused to have her name inscribed in the Francesca family mausoleum, something that everyone in the local village had found distasteful.

Detective Inspector King was becoming more and more interested in the case and was certain that Madeleine and Evelyn would be excited to hear the news.

Something else that was making Alastair King more and more interested was Madeleine herself. She was an enigma and he felt happy and nervous and giddy with excitement every time he was near her. She never spoke much to him, allowing Evelyn to do most of the talking, but he had noticed her gazing at him on several occasions. It never made him feel nervous, but his heart galloped and missed a beat whenever she was near. He felt like an electric charge had been sparked between them and he was more than just a little enthusiastic to be taking this trip to Italy with her.

He knocked on the door of the castle and was surprised to see that Madeleine was there to welcome him in. He was unaware that Evelyn was also sensing the interest that Madeleine and Alastair had of each other and was playing cupid by trying to get the two to talk to each other.

"Good morning Detective Inspector King, please come in." smiled Madeleine.

"Good morning Mademoiselle, thank you. I hope you are well?" asked Alastair as he entered the castle.

Madeleine shyly replied that she was well and that her and Evelyn were so looking forward to his news. Leading Detective Inspector King to the library, where Evelyn was waiting for them, the two fell silent, not knowing what to say.

"Good morning Detective Inspector King!" Evelyn exclaimed excitedly. "Please have a seat, we are so excited to hear your news!"

Alastair took a seat opposite the two women and began to explain the details of the letter that he'd received from Massimo the day before.

"So, ladies, if you'd like to take a trip to Italy for a few days, I would be very happy to accompany you and learn more about this case." said Alastair, smiling broadly as he saw the two women's faces light up in happiness.

They decided to make the arrangements that very day and leave the following morning for Italy. It was a rather large undertaking to arrange all the details, but they began as soon as Detective Inspector King left, promising to meet at the village train station at nine a.m. the next morning. Evelyn had decided to make life a little simpler and not take her ladies maid with her. She would travel light and only pack one trunk of luggage. She knew how to dress and arrange her hair herself and felt like it would end up being more bother to have attendants trailing along with them. They would only be there for a few days, and she could manage everything herself whilst abroad.

Chapter 13

Arriving at their accommodations, after a tiring journey to Italy, the trio unpacked, supped and had a good night's rest. Early the next morning, the plan was to meet with Massimo, Detective Inspector King's friend, who would then take them to the retired Italian police detective, Marco Gotti, who had worked on Isabella's case. Marco lived relatively close to Count Vincenzo Francesca's Lake Como villa.

Sitting in his living room, waiting for his guests to arrive, Marco had his still very active mind run through the case as he remembered it. He had also pulled the case file, something he'd taken with him when he retired, to make sure he hadn't forgotten any details, but he knew he hadn't. He had always had his suspicions about the Count and the events of that night that ended with the death of his wife. The account that Count Francesca had given, just hadn't added up, but with lack of any evidence to prove otherwise, the detectives working the case had to simply rely on their only eye witness to the tragedy – the Count's.

It had been such a sad case and after all these years, it still felt unresolved for Marco, even though officially, the case had been closed after a very short-lived investigation.

Arriving at the door of Marco Gotti's residence, Alastair, Madeleine, Evelyn and Massimo knocked and waited for the door to be answered. Madeleine and Evelyn were extremely nervous about what was in store for them today. What if the information that they were about to receive was the opposite of what they believed happened to Isabella? That would have devastating consequences because that would mean Isabella's spirit might never leave them alone and never be at peace. Palms sweaty and feeling a little flustered, they entered the home of Marco Gotti, who had greeted them so warmly at the door.

"Please, sit down," said Marco, smiling and gesturing to the living room chairs.

At first, Marco and Massimo chatted excitedly and spoke of days long gone when they had met and become friends. Before long, the conversation turned to the matter at hand.

"Tell us your feeling involving this case Marco," prompted Alastair.

"Well, the facts of the case are as follows... Count Vincenzo Francesca and his new bride, Isabella, were on board a vessel, headed for England, on their honeymoon. Apparently, the Countess slipped when her and her husband were on deck, alone. She fell overboard and the alarm was raised by the Count, however, by the time the crew was on deck, she had already sunk beneath the surface, and no one was ever able to bring her body back up. My feelings on the situation were that it didn't add up. I can't put my finger on it, but I do remember asking myself how she'd sunk so quickly, as the Count had assured us at the time that he had alerted for help immediately as soon as she hit the water. Most people who drown or even get dragged under by their clothing, of which she was wearing a heavy floor length gown, would have spluttered and struggled for a few moments before sinking so comprehensively that there is no sight of them. That has always been a nagging thought for me for many years now.

"Well, I think we should go and see this Count Francesca and see what he can uncover," said Alastair, rising to his feet.

"My thoughts exactly," said Marco.

Looking down from the roadside, sat the sprawling estate, built on the side of a sheer cliff, overlooking the stunningly beautiful Lake Como. It was a breath-taking scene. The sun was shining down beautifully, and the smell of jasmine wafted in the light breeze, which moved around the parklike gardens. It had so many beautiful flowers, such as hibiscus, frangipani, and the jasmine that they had smelled, as well as plants like delicious monster, were everywhere around a beautifully manicured lawn leading up to the huge double doors of the villa.

The lake itself was shimmering like quicksilver in the sunlight and the group were quite taken aback at the sheer natural beauty of this place.

Approaching the property, the group walked up to the front door, led by Marco Gotti. He used the giant lions head door knocker on the magnificent, large, double, intricately carved, wooden doors. They could hear the locks on the door being unbolted and the door opened. A man was standing there but was immediately recognised to be the Count's butler.

"Buongiorno, Sir, we are here to see Count Francesca, please." said Marco.

The door simply closed on them and after a few moments, the butler reappeared and ushered them into the villa. He led them through a large entrance hall and into a beautifully decorated living room which they presumed looked over the lake, although they could not tell, as all the heavy curtains were drawn tightly shut and for all its beauty, the room was dark, cold and smelled musty, like it was in dire need of an airing.

There was a fire roaring in the fireplace, even though the

weather was glorious outside and above the fireplace, hung an enormous portrait of a young women, which Madeleine recognised immediately as Isabella. She nudged Evelyn and discreetly pointed towards the portrait, feeling surprised that the Count would have this portrait in such a prominent place, if he was truly to blame for her death, as they had suspected. They did not realise that the Count had long been playing the part of the sorrowful, grieving husband, even when he had married his other two wives. He liked to keep the portrait of Isabella in full view of anyone who might be visiting the villa, in order to gather as much sympathy, and at the same time, cast away any lurking suspicions that he had anything to do with his first wife's death. He often thought to himself that, perhaps, this was the reason that he continued to be haunted by his long dead wife, every waking moment.

Sitting in an armchair, facing the fire, they noticed the Count and approached him.

"Count Francesca, please allow us to introduce ourselves," started Marco Gotti, "I'm not sure if you remember me from so many years ago, but I was the investigating officer on the case of your wife's unfortunate death. Marco Gotti." He extended his hand, which was ignored by the Count. "These are my friends, Detective Inspector Massimo Furnarello, Detective Inspector Alastair King, Lady Evelyn Beauchamp and Mademoiselle Madeleine de Longpre."

"What do you people want?" snarled Vincenzo.

"We wish to speak to you about your late first wife, Isabella." Said Marco flatly, remembering his distinct dislike for the Count all those years ago and feeling the same repulsion again now.

Sighing, the count looked detached and disinterested. "That

was a very long time ago and I don't not wish to dredge dead wives up now!" said the count, callously.

Shocked at this retort, the ladies gasped and that made the old Count laugh. He knew very well that there was no way in hell that any evidence of him doing anything to Isabella would be found. He did not need to discuss this again.

"Sir," pleaded Evelyn, "we have had some disturbing occurrences recently and that has forced our hand in coming to speak with you. Please just listen to what we have to say."

Becoming annoyed, the Count rose from his chair. "Hear this, I have no interest in discussing Isabella or what happened to her! Furthermore, I neither care nor am I interested in whatever these so-called disturbing occurrences are!" he boomed, getting angrier by the minute.

He was old, frail and stooped over, but still a commanding presence. He slowly turned away from the group before they could utter another word, calling for his butler to show these uninvited guests off the property. Suddenly, the light and the room shifted, and on the walls, there were shafts of light dancing in wavy patterns, much like rays of light streaming into water. Madeleine noticed them immediately and everything seemed to slow down and the voices of the others trying to convince the Count to speak with them echoed in her ears. Her palms became sweaty, and she instinctively put a hand onto Evelyn's arm to steady herself. Evelyn, noticing immediately that Madeleine was looking ashen, got the attention of Detective Inspector King, who in turn, helped Madeleine onto the sofa to sit and compose herself. Detective Inspector King sat down next to her, as everyone began to notice what was going on. The Count had a confused look on his face. Detective Inspector King took Madeleine's hand to comfort her and as soon as their hands touched, they both felt an electric charge spark between them. They let go of each other for a moment, looked into each other's eyes and then Detective Inspector King slipped his hand back into Madeleine's and smiled. She longed to bask in this moment with Alastair, but it was not enough to distract her from what was happening around her. The Count was now complaining bitterly that they needed to leave, completely oblivious to the changing energy in the room. He was pacing up and down, trying to get them to leave, when he suddenly stopped in his tracks, a look of pure terror on his face. The group all turned towards the large, curtained windows where the Count was focusing all his attention.

Isabella was standing there, her eyes locked with the Count's. He was gasping for air, beginning to hyperventilate. "No! NO!" he screamed. She did not move. Everyone was bearing silent witness to this exchange between the Count and his long dead wife.

Isabella had a look of wrath on her face, her head tilted slightly forward, black eyes seemingly boring into the Count's soul. The room began to get darker and shake as though a violent earthquake was occurring. Ornaments and glasses were being flung off the tables and smashing to the floor, the crystal chandelier above them began to swing back and forth and the portrait of Isabella shook so violently that it came off the wall and fell to the ground. The Count's face was twisted in fear and agony, he clutched his chest. "I'm sorry Isabella, please, I'm sorry!" he was shouting to her over the deafening thunder emanating from Isabella.

In an instant, he fell to the ground in a crumpled heap. Marco and Massimo ran to his side to assist him. The Count's face was grey, sweaty and distorted. He had a look of pure terror, and he couldn't move or speak. The group soon realised that he was having a heart attack. Massimo began unbuttoning the Count's shirt and releasing his tie once he'd turned Vincenzo onto his back on the floor. He began to pump on Vincenzo's chest and give him mouth to mouth, all the while, Vincenzo seemed to be slipping away. The group was in a frenzy trying to aid the Count but soon, he seemed to gasp one last time and then stopped. Marco felt for a pulse. "He's dead!" he declared, looking at each of them, disbelievingly. Instantly, the noise, the darkness, the shaking ceased.

At that, they all looked at Isabella, she seemed to be transforming before their very eyes.

No longer before them, stood that terrifying apparition, but the beautiful woman that she had once been. Healthy, vibrant and full of life, she was smiling at them.

"Isabella…" murmured Madeleine. Isabella turned her gaze on Madeleine and lifted one finger to her lips to hush Madeleine. Slowly, she seemed to vanish and in the blink of an eye, she was gone. The group could immediately hear the birdsong outside and felt the room become warm again.

Dumbfounded, they walked out of the villa, after instructing the butler that they would be sending the doctor and the police back to the villa. They went to the police station with Massimo and Marco to file their statements on what had occurred, all agreeing that nothing would be said about the apparition.

Madeleine felt lighter and happier than she had since she first began her journey from France to visit Highclere Castle.

The feeling of seasickness was completely gone, and she felt great, an enormous weight having been lifted from her shoulders. Walking towards the police station with the group,

Alastair walked next to her, allowing the others to go ahead, all excitedly discussing what they had just witnessed. It was clear to all of them, that the Count had indeed murdered his wife and that Isabella had finally had her revenge and was now at peace.

Alastair looked at Madeleine walking beside him and when she noticed him looking at her, they smiled. Silently, he took her hand in his and they walked silently down the hill to their destination.

Chapter 14

Once the Italian police had given their permission for the group to leave, after giving their statements, they decided to stay in Italy for a few days before returning to England. They all deserved a little holiday after all the terror and excitement of the past week and the next morning, Evelyn came running down the stairs excitedly, announcing that her husband, Malcolm had decided to join them in Italy for the last two days of their trip on his way back to England from his business trip.

"It'll be like a couple's holiday!" exclaimed Evelyn, winking at Madeleine, who immediately felt herself blushing. The night before, Alastair had been attentive to her, but they had not yet had a chance to discuss their blatantly obvious budding romance. Evelyn was beyond excited for the two of them and couldn't wait for Malcolm to arrive so that she wouldn't feel like an intruder on Madeleine and Alastair's romance.

Alastair was happy to have Malcolm arriving that afternoon, so that he could spend some time with Madeleine on their own. He had fallen head over heels for her, something he'd never felt before and was determined to see how she felt about him. That evening, the foursome went for dinner at an old Italian restaurant that was recommended to them by the locals. The views were spectacular, overlooking the lake in the early evening. The smells of the delicious food, mixing with the fragrance of the flowers which hung in baskets along the stone patio of the restaurant was intoxicating and very romantic. They told Malcolm all about their adventure as they dined on a variety of pastas and drank heady, aromatic wine from the local vineyard. Madeleine was still feeling very shy around Alastair. She'd never been in a romantic relationship before and suddenly felt awkward and tongue-tied. Evelyn was so happy to have Malcolm with her again that she spent most of the time, doting on her husband and cooing in his ear. After a long and lazy dinner, they began to walk back to the villa where they were staying, in pairs of two. Alastair took Madeleine's hand and slowed her down, enough so that Evelyn and Malcolm were out of ear shot. "Can we talk?" he asked, nervously, gazing into Madeleine's eyes. Madeleine stopped and looked up into Alastair's handsome face and felt her heart beginning to flutter.

Walking ahead, Evelyn glanced back at them, and noticing what was happening, she smiled, "I think we should leave them for a while" she said and promptly linked her arm through her husband's and took him home so that they could have their own romantic time at the villa.

The sun was just beginning to set, and the sky was showing off in all its glory, glowing in pinks, reds and oranges. There was a bench on the side of the road, overlooking the lake and Alastair steered Madeleine towards it. They both sat down in silence for a few moments, still admiring the scenery.

At last, Alastair looked over at Madeleine and sensing he was about to speak, she turned and looked into his beautiful blue eyes. There were butterflies in her stomach doing somersaults and she was nervous and exhilarated at the same time.

"What have you done to me Madeleine?" he asked, seriously.

Startled, she immediately replied, "Why, what's wrong Alastair?" worried that he thought she'd put some kind of love spell on him.

"Do you mean, what's right? Madeleine, I have never felt this way before. Since the moment I first locked eyes with you, I could hear my heart whisper to me, and that voice has just been getting louder and lounder. I'm consumed by you. You're all I can think of every minute of every day."

"I too have never felt this way about anyone before," Madeleine admitted. That seemed to put Alastair at ease, and he smiled down at her. They gazed into each other's eyes for a long while, the stunning scenery completely forgotten.

Then, a cloud seemed to pass over Alastair's face, and he asked, "When do you have to go back to France?"

Sadly, Madeleine had been thinking about this all day and did not yet want to face reality. A long-distance relationship would be hard, and she wasn't sure that they were prepared for it.

"I was scheduled to leave for France right after the week of séances at Highclere Castle," she said sadly, "but I do not have anything pressing in France that I need to return to immediately." Hopeful that he would ask her to stay in England a while longer once they got back.

"Please don't go back right away…" whispered Alastair, looking longingly into her eyes.

"I'm not sure that Evelyn and her family's hospitality will allow me to stay much longer at Highclere Castle. Malcolm has returned and Evelyn will be going back to London to her own home."

"Stay in the village for a while. I have some more vacation time owing to me and I could show you around and you and I could get to know each other a bit better," he said excitedly, silently willing Madeleine to take this leap of faith with him.

"Or" exclaimed Madeleine, "you could come with me to France for your holidays…" Please say yes, please say yes, she said over and over in her mind.

"That is a fantastic idea! I have never been to France, but I will only come if you promise me that you will spend every waking moment with me and show me everything you love about France," he said, smiling at Madeleine.

"Of course, it would be my pleasure!" she smiled.

He slowly put his finger under her chin and lifted her face to his. He bent forward and kissed her, a kiss so tender and sweet that she felt like she was melting into a puddle on the floor.

The End